Imalee walked softly across the room, "Poor little Gregor. Do you have a headache? Would you like for me to make it better?"

"Leave me alone!" Gregor jerked back, knocking his chair over as he stood, and walked away from the wizard's soft hands.

Imalee laughed, "You are so worried about your people. What will you give me to fix their problems?" The soft voice held more than a hint of cruelty.

Gregor stopped, his back to the wizard. Tears ran down his young face; his thin shoulders drooped. "Anything," he whispered, fear and revulsion in his voice.

"My sweet emperor-to-be, I did not hear your answer. What is the well-being of your people worth?" The soft hands touched the back of Gregor's neck.

Gregor bowed his head, "I will do anything you require of me, Wizard Imalee." The young man replied, defeated.

The Weeping Crystal

Aruda Hanna Wilson

*Best Wishes
Aruda Hanna Wilson*

Deer Hawk Enterprises
Florida

The Weeping Crystal
Copyright © 2008 by Aruda Hanna Wilson

All rights reserved. No part of this publication may be reproduced, stored in a retrieval system or transmitted in any form or by any means, electronic, mechanical, photocopying, recording or otherwise without prior written permission of the copyright owner except for excerpts quoted in the context of reviews.

This is a work of fiction. Names, characters, places and incidents portrayed in this book are either the product of the author's imagination or are used fictitiously. Any resemblance to actual persons, living or dead, events or locales is entirely coincidental.

Cover design by:
Sandra Takaro-Miller

Layout by:
Aurelia Sands

Published by:
Deer Hawk Enterprises
www.deerhawkpublications.com
Library of Congress Control Number:
2008924990

Printed in the United States of America

The author wishes to thank all the family, friends and friendly strangers who have offered encouragement over the years.
To my god-daughter Kara, special thanks, and, of course, to my lovely editor who just presented me with a grandson: I couldn't have done without you both; my husband for tolerating my bouts of frenzied writing and my children who finally realized that love meant cooking for themselves.
A. Hanna Wilson

Prologue

In the days of long ago, before the time of written history, four beings, fleeing war in their own dimension, came to the world of Taron. They found this new world pleasing to them and decided to stay. These four beings were Stone and Storm, two males, and Crystal and Mist, two females.

Stone, a tall, dark-haired, green-eyed being and the fiery red-haired, brown-eyed Crystal, were life mates, but Storm envied them and was determined to have Crystal for his own. Gray-eyed Mist loved the black-eyed, blond Storm, and when she saw the way his envy twisted his soul and darkened his heart, it caused her great pain. She tried to warn Stone and Crystal about

Storm's feelings, but they did not take her warning seriously, for they could not believe Storm would betray them.

Mist lived in the high places. On clear days, all who looked could see her smoke-colored hair swirling as she danced among the mountain peaks in the north of Taron's eastern continent. She had very little dealings with the humans of this new world, but she would visit her friends Crystal and Stone, and they knew that she would always help them if needed.

Taron had two main continents, one in the east, and one in the west. Stone loved the wild desert of the eastern continent, and the hardy men and women who lived there. He taught the men strong warrior magic, and they worshipped him as the god of war. Gradually under Stone's influence, all the tribes came together under a leader specially blessed by Stone, called the Ah'Jarl, 'He who protects.' The desert was named Stoneland, in honor of Stone.

Crystal settled among the gentle people of the eastern continent's plains. Their women controlled the villages while the men went out to farm, fish, and hunt. She named the most powerful witch of each generation Holder of the

Crystal Throne, the one who was to lead her people. Crystal taught the men how to carve the crystal and silver mined from the northern mountains, and they created buildings and statues of unearthly beauty. She taught the women, both of the plains and the desert, woman's magic, a magic that dealt with life in all its cycles. The people worshipped her as an incarnation of the moon goddess. The plains were called Crystia, and its capitol was Crystal City in honor of Crystal.

Storm took the whole western continent and molded the men there in his own image, making them despise their women as weak and useless. He gathered the strongest of the dark souls he could find, and formed them into the first Wizard Council. Storm then moved against Crystal and Stone by sending a message to Stone in Crystal's name. When Stone arrived at the meeting place, Storm captured and bound him deep in the desert.

"Here you will stay," Storm intoned, as his power swirled around him, "Until the sun no longer shines." Just as Storm was about to close his spell, Mist slid in.

"Here you remain until the desert and the plains are one."

Storm was furious, but it was too late for him to stop the magic, so he sealed Stone in the earth, then turned his attention to Crystal. But she, sensing what had happened, fled Crystal City and joined Mist in the high mountains. Mist hid the weeping Crystal from Storm.

Mist took a lock of Crystal's hair, set it in a cave, and charged Frya, the queen of Crystia's sister, and her descendents to guard it. Mist then wrapped her essence around the mountain, hiding the cave from all but Frya. Frya moved her family to the mountains, where they lived ever since. After that, Mist had no more dealings with the people of Taron.

For a while, Storm raged across the eastern continent, looking for Crystal. At last, he gave up and returned to his own lands. Before he left, however, he planted deep mistrust between the people of Stone and Crystal. Each blamed the other for betraying their god.

Storm sent his wizards to live among the people of the Crystia to guarantee that the war between the neighbors would go on until the ties to their gods weakened and Storm could rule the whole world of Taron, claiming Crystal for his own.

Chapter One

"Whose child is she?" The large, dark-haired man snarled.

"Mine! And that makes her heir to the Crystal Throne. There is nothing you and your wizards from the west can do about that. The Crystal Throne will always be ruled over by a woman." The tall, slender woman turned to look at her companion, "Richard, what makes you think she is not your daughter?"

"The wizards have told me. My seed breeds only males."

"Oh, poor Richard! Your masculinity is diminished by fathering a daughter? This is Crystia; the queens of this land bear only daughters."

"You lie!"

"Hear me, Man of the Western Lands, I did not choose you as mate. I am the holder of the Crystal Throne. Call me a liar ever again and you and your accursed wizards will die by my own hands if needed. This child is the heir to my throne and none of you may gainsay her. She is borne of my body, and it will not shame me, but it will shame you if you deny her."

"Katria, you will rue this day, I swear it."

With that, Richard stormed out of the room, slamming the door behind him.

*****

"Katria, may I see the baby?" The voice came from a man standing on the balcony.

"Marical, are you insane? What if Richard had seen you?"

The tall man with dark, brown eyes laughed, "Beloved, when are you going to realize that I am House Frya? No one sees me unless I wish them to."

"Oh shut up and come in. The window is unlocked." Katria moved to the baby and picked her up.

"Look at her. Isn't she beautiful? She looks a little like you."

"I hope not. Richard is not a fool, and he is already suspicious." Marical smiled.

Katria shrugged, "We are cousins. That nose is a House Frya trademark. What shall we name her?"

Marical was silent for a long moment, "Crystal has named her, Mar'ya Olena, 'she who will bring light into darkness'."

Marical studied Katria carefully, "Katria are you well?"

Katria smiled, "Dearheart, I am well. This child is necessary. I knew that giving birth to her might cost my life, but Crystal demanded it, and she gave me the strength to survive. Look at her, Marical: The future of our people, so tiny and innocent."

Katria and Marical looked at the child, then Marical touched the baby's cheek. "I must leave now."

"Marical, does Alana know?"

"Yes, she and the children know, but they are House Frya. They will tell no one, and will protect Mar'ya with their lives."

"Tell Alana I am sorry."

"Are you?"

"No. Not sorry that you and I loved each other, but sorry that it led to us betraying Alana."

"Katria, Alana and I both love you as much as you love Alana and I. We will not meet again, but know that I love you and I love our daughter. Farewell."

Marical stepped out the window and disappeared into the darkness.

*****

"Katria, where are you and the child going?" Belia Sultav, Queen Mother, demanded.

"The child has a name, Mother. Mar'ya is three, and it is time she visited the mountains of Frya."

"Why? Why do you still hold with those outdated customs? The wizards have proven those customs useless. The only reason you have for visiting Frya is to see Marical Qualdar again."

"Mother, Marical is dying. I know you do not care. After all, he is only a man who serves Crystal and not one of the westerners. Your love for the westerners is legendary. I do not understand it, nor do I share it. You have forced me to wed one of them, and the future will judge you harshly for that. You have abdicated the Crystal Throne to me. I am queen now. You have no say in my actions."

"You listen to me young woman: I had a small, sickly child whose father was so involved with his stupid, antiquated religion that he didn't have time for me or you. I found you a strong man who would support you, and not abandon you, like your father did me. I abdicated so that you and Richard could rule together; I did not expect you to shut him out the way you have. If there are problems in the future, then history will judge it your fault for humiliating that proud man. I don't understand how you could be so cruel to that sweet man." Belia stared at her daughter with narrowed eyes. "I did not raise you to be so cold and unfeeling. After all I have done for you, you treat me just like your father did. You ask why I like the westerners? It is because they understand my gentle sensibilities. I should never have allowed your father to take you to House Frya," Belia blinked rapidly.

Katria laughed, "Don't try to bring tears to your eyes, Mother, I know you far better than you think. You didn't care when I went to

House Frya to live, you were glad to get rid of me. My father expected you to act like the queen of Crystia, not some useless, pampered western female. When you discovered that you could not manipulate him with your tears and your fluttering hands, you threw both of us out. 'Take your sickly child and return to Frya.' Those were your exact words. In the twenty years I spent at House Frya, you never contacted me." Katria paused, took a deep breath, then continued, "Belia, once queen of Crystia, return to your rooms and bother me no more. I have spoken." Katria, holder of the Crystal Throne, took her daughter's hand and walked to the waiting carriage.

*****

Far across the ocean to the west, a thirteen-year-old boy sat alone at a large table. His dark-blue eyes were full of anger, and his hands on the table before him were clenched.

"Gregor, what have you done?" A hesitant female voice asked softly.

"Mother, go to your rooms. If you are found in the main palace you will be put to death." Gregor's voice was harsh.

"I have permission from Wizard Rede to speak with you," she whispered.

"This is none of your concern." Gregor sighed. "Leave me alone like you and my father have always done."

"Do you think I have acted this way from choice?" The hint of tears in her voice made Gregor tense. "Gregor, be careful. If you anger the priests and the wizards, you will die."

"Like my half-brother Adam?"

"Gregor! Don't say that. Don't even think it." His mother admonished. "I loved Adam as if he were my own son. I raised him after his mother died in childbirth." Her voice dropped to a whisper, "I warned him to be careful around the wizards and the priests. I warned him."

"Woman what are you doing here?" A soft, male voice interrupted from the door.

"She is my mother, Merle of Arnus, and first wife of the emperor. Wizard Imalee, be careful how you speak to her." Gregor snarled.

"I have permission, mighty wizard. Wizard Rede gave me leave to speak with my son," she said softly.

"I see. Have you spoken to your son?"

"Yes." The woman bowed her head.

"Then leave."

Merle gave a desperate glance at her son and fled the room.

Imalee turned to Gregor, "I hear you left the palace without permission today." He said mildly.

"I'm sure you also heard that I was not happy with what I saw: The priests in their great, ornate houses, and the churches covered with gold, while the people starve in the streets." Gregor closed his eyes.

"That is none of your concern."

"I will be emperor someday. My father left his people in your care while he cavorts with the whores of the east. Tell me, when he returns and sees how well you and the priests have not cared for them, how will he react?"

"You are not emperor yet, you are just a little boy." Imalee chuckled.

Gregor shook his head, "Don't. Don't threaten me. I have read the charter. The priests are charged by the god to protect and strengthen his children so that, when the time comes, we can descend upon the eastern lands like locusts and devour them. The starving masses outside the palace will most likely devour themselves before we ever reach the land of our god's enemy."

"Where did you find a copy of the charter?" Imalee asked sharply.

"In your rooms," Gregor answered, as he rubbed between his eyes.

Imalee walked softly across the room, "Poor little Gregor. Do you have a headache? Would you like for me to make it better?"

"Leave me alone!" Gregor jerked back, knocking his chair over as he stood, and walked away from the wizard's soft hands.

Imalee laughed, "You are so worried about your people. What will you give me to fix their problems?" The soft voice held more than a hint of cruelty.

Gregor stopped, his back to the wizard. Tears ran down his young face; his thin shoulders drooped. "Anything," he whispered, fear and revulsion in his voice.

"My sweet emperor-to-be, I did not hear your answer. What is the well-being of your people worth?" The soft hands touched the back of Gregor's neck.

Gregor bowed his head, "I will do anything you require of me, Wizard Imalee." The young man replied, defeated.

A heavily veiled figure moved swiftly away from where it was listening outside the door. Merle of Arnus, first wife of Richard, twenty-sixth emperor of the western empire, and mother of the heir, wept. A soft litany came from behind her veil, "I hate them; I hate the wizards. Oh my son."

Chapter Two

"I'm bored, Rowan. Tell me more stories of Crystal." Mar'ya leaned her head on her cousin's shoulder.

"Imp, I told you all the stories I know, you have to ask Mother or Solari for more stories." Ten-year-old Rowan grinned down at Mar'ya.

"Solari is busy, let's go find Gail. She always has lots of stories." Mar'ya jumped to her feet and tugged Rowan's hand, "Come on, hurry, get up."

Rowan laughed and stood, "You are in such a hurry. Slow down, Imp."

"Rowan, why do you and Gail call me Imp? Is that a bad thing?"

Rowan dropped to her knees and hugged the tiny three-year-old, "Oh Mar'ya, we love you. You are so small and so full of energy, always bouncing around, just like a little Imp."

"I'm an Imp because you love me?"

"Yes." Rowan stood and took Mar'ya's hand, "You are an Imp because we love you."

Mar'ya thought about that for a minute then nodded, "That's all right. If it means you love me, I'll let you call me Imp."

The two little girls skipped down the corridor to their older cousin's room. Rowan tapped softly on the door. "Gail, are you in? Mar'ya and I want more stories please."

The door opened to reveal a tall, thin, serious twelve-year-old, "Come in. Solari is here with her new boyfriend and some other of her friends."

Mar'ya wrinkled her tiny nose, "They are from the desert. Ugh! My daddy says they are all savages." She paused, a frown creasing her forehead, "What is a savage, Gail?"

"A savage is anyone who doesn't agree with your daddy. Anyway, Alex is a cousin, and he is really cute."

Mar'ya peeped around Gail and sighed, "Does that mean no stories tonight?"

Solari laughed, "Come in girls. I'm leaving, so you can visit with Gail."

"Okay." Mar'ya said happily and squeezed past Gail into the room. A young boy about her age stood between a nomad woman and Solari's boyfriend. He and Mar'ya stared at each other, then he crossed his eyes and stuck his tongue out at her. Mar'ya giggled, tried to mimic the boy's actions, failed and laughed even harder. She walked up to him and wrinkled her nose.

"You smell bad." She announced.

"I'm supposed to smell bad. I'm a boy." The other child announced with lofty disdain.

Mar'ya stared at him, then glanced around the room, trying to find someone to disprove his statement, "Shen doesn't smell bad." She said dubiously, as she caught sight of Shen sitting quietly in a corner.

Both children turned and stared at Shen, "Shen is sixteen, he's almost grown up." The lad replied.

Mar'ya nodded understandingly. "It would be super if I had someone my own age to play with, and I like you. Are you staying with us?"

"No, I have to go home with my mother." He gave her a gap-toothed grin. "Maybe Aunt Solari can bring you to play with me at my house." He looked hopefully at Solari.

"Maybe someday," Solari smiled gently at the two disappointed faces staring at her. Both children knew that phrase meant never.

Mar'ya drooped her shoulders dramatically, stared curiously at three adult strangers in the room, then she shrugged. "Are you savages?" She asked the woman.

"Mar'ya that is not polite." Gail admonished. "Apologize at once."

Mar'ya, moved close to the Nomad woman, and took a deep breath, "You smell good, like fresh air. I like you. But Gail said that savages are people that don't agree with daddy, so I want to know if you are savages." Mar'ya explained with impeccable three-year-old logic.

"Well that makes us all savages." Solari murmured, as the adults laughed

"Me too," Mar'ya added smiling happily at the friendly faces around her.

When the adults left the room, Mar'ya curled up on the floor and stared thoughtfully at Gail. "Gail?"

"Yes, Mar'ya?"

"I like that boy; I wish I could have introduced him to Crystal. When I grow up can I have him for my boyfriend?"

Gail chocked back a laugh, "What do you know about boyfriends?"

"Well you said that Alex is Solari's boyfriend and he was cute."

"Oh, so you think that young man was cute?" Gail smiled

"No, but he can cross his eyes. That's better than being cute." Mar'ya replied with great conviction.

She waited until Gail stopped laughing before tugging on her hand, "Story, now," she demanded.

"Lessons first, story later." Gail said sternly, standing up and leading Mar'ya to House Frya's chapel.

"Okay." Mar'ya skipped beside her tall cousin. Gail taught her fun things, like never letting a wizard touch her head. "I never want to go back to the place where all the stinky wizards live." She giggled, "Gail, why do the wizards always smell so bad?"

"What?"

"Well, everyone here smells like fresh air. Even the people from the desert smell good, but the wizards smell like old mops." Mar'ya explained seriously.

"I don't know. I have never been that close to a wizard. They are not allowed on House Frya lands. Have you been studying history with Shen?" Gail carefully avoided the question.

"No. He is sooo booring, I always fall asleep." Mar'ya admitted cheerfully.

"Oh dear," Gail sighed, "Mar'ya you are going to be queen someday. Don't you think it would be nice to know the history of your people?"

"Yes, I'll ask Crystal."

"Crystal talks to you?"

"Yes," the tiny head nodded vigorously, "But I am not allowed to tell anyone what she says. It's a secret." Mar'ya touched Gail's arm, "Gail, she is so sad, why don't you tell her a story and cheer her up?"

"Do you think that would work?" Gail asked as she studied the child next to her.

"Yes. I told her that you are really good at telling stories, so she said she wants you to come and tell her all your stories."

Gail stared in astonishment at Mar'ya's proclamation, then turned to face the lock of Crystal's hair kept in the temple. Tears ran down her face.

"Gail, did I do something wrong?" Mar'ya asked worriedly.

"No, I am very happy. You just told me that Crystal has chosen me to be the next Mistress of House Frya." Gail knelt before the shimmering crystal.

Mar'ya smiled. She was glad that her older cousin was happy. "I told her you would be the bestest person in the whole world for the job." The three-year-old said smugly.

*****

"Mar'ya Olena, your mother will be here soon."

"Yes, Aunt Alana. I just want to visit Crystal once more. Please."

Alana Oran, Mistress of House Frya and Guardian of the Burning Crystal, smiled at the sturdy five-year-old. "You sound so grown up. Relax, Little One, there is plenty of time. You should enjoy being a child. Go out and spend time with Rowan, then go to visit Crystal; I'll call you when your mother arrives."

"No, I don't have a lot of time. I must grow up soon, Crystal has spoken. Oops, that's supposed to be a secret." Worried dark-brown eyes stared up at Alana.

"I will keep your secret, Mar'ya. I am very good at keeping secrets."

"I love you this much, Aunt Alana." Small arms stretched out to their limit as Mar'ya gave a big grin showing two missing front teeth.

"Oh Mar'ya, I am going to miss you so much when you leave."

"Do I have to go, Aunt Alana?"

"Yes. Your destiny lies in the city, but remember that House Frya will always claim you as theirs." Alana hugged the little body close, then stared into the eyes that were so like her husband's. "I love you very much, true daughter of Crystia. Now you must go and spend time with your cousins, then you can visit Crystal."

*****

"Katria, you look so frail. What is happening in the city?" Alana frowned at her young cousin. "Come over here and sit down while I send for a hot drink."

Katria sighed, "I am so tired, Alana. I wish I could stay in these mountains forever."

"Are Belia and Richard making problems?" Alana took Katria's hands in hers. "Oh Crystal, Katria you are so cold. Here, move closer to fire."

"Want to switch places with me? I'll stay here; you go to the city and cope with Belia and Richard." Katria gave a small smile. "Don't worry. Crystal has promised that I will live long enough to present Mar'ya."

"What happens after that? Katria, Mar'ya will only be twelve when you leave her. That is too young. Richard and the wizards will destroy her."

"You and Crystal had her for the last two years, Alana. We can only hope and pray you laid a strong enough foundation. Neither of us will live long enough to see her claim her heritage. You know that, don't you?"

Alana closed her eyes and bowed her head, "Seer and queen, we will join Crystal, and with Marical. We will watch our daughter grow strong and wise."

Katria touched Alana's gray hair and smiled, "When did you get so old, Beloved?"

"I'm sixty. Twenty-five years older than you."

"I keep forgetting. You and Marical always seemed so young. Alana, did you hate me when Mar'ya was born?"

"Katria, both Marical and I loved you. We both knew that you loved us; I was honored that you chose Marical to father the child of prophecy. Mar'ya is a sweet, loving child, and I love her as if she had been born of my body."

Katria wrinkled her nose at Alana, "I fell in love with your husband when I was eight years old."

"Yes, I remember. You walked into the sitting room and announced that you were going to marry both of us as soon as you were old enough."

"Well, I knew if I wanted him, I would have to take you as well." Katria giggled. "So, the children have met?" She added after a moment.

"Yes, it went well. Katria, why did you insist on that meeting?"

"One day, they will need each other's trust. It will be a difficult time. I hope the memory of this meeting will help them win through." Katria sighed, "It's difficult to be a prophet. The images are so blurred. All I do is hope the decisions I make are correct."

"I don't think they will remember this meeting."

"They will remember at some level. All we can do now, is hope."

Alana hugged Katria, "Relax, Little One, let House Frya pamper you for a while. There is no rush to return to the city. Rest here for a while."

Katria sighed in contentment, "Alana, you must send Shen to the city soon. Mar'ya will need him."

Alana laughed, "He is only fifteen, and trying to single-handedly repopulate House Frya."

Katria snickered, "'Hand' is not the word I would use." She leaned back in her chair and fell asleep.

*****

"The girl is almost a woman. It is time we found a mate for her." Richard glanced at his wife's thin, pale face.

"Richard, Mar'ya Olena is still a child. She is only ten and has not yet been approved by Crystal and the people of Crystia. We will not, I repeat, will not, raise her as one of your useless western women. The Crystal Guardians shall choose her mate."

"You are an idiot. Why do you insist on all these barbaric customs? Your mother understood that the world is changing. If Crystia wants to continue to exist in the new world, you will have to get rid of these outmoded notions."

"My mother has been dead for three years. I am nothing like her, or didn't you notice? Listen well, Richard of the West: For over a thousand years, your wizards have been hovering over Crystia like vultures waiting for us to die. We have not died, nor will my people roll over and submit to your rule."

Richard smiled, "I wonder how many of your House Lords would agree with you? They realize, even if you don't, that it is not natural for women to rule over men."

Katria turned away from his smile, "Richard, I will try to explain: The House Lords may be seduced, but the people revere Crystal. The people: The faceless, loving, loyal, farmer, hunter, fisherman, and miner are the ones who support Crystal. House Lords were something your wizards devised to separate our people. No matter what you do, the old ways will return."

Richard laughed, "You always were a sickly, hysterical woman. Your House Lords recognize that. No one believes in that old garbage anymore. It is a dying religion, one fit only for weaklings and women."

Katria heard the trace of unease in Richard's laughter and smiled. "Richard, Lord of the Western Lands, hear me: Before I allow my country to become one of your western city states, I would bury it in the sands of the desert."

Chapter Three

Twelve-year-old Mar'ya stared at her reflection in the tall mirror, tried to cross her eyes, and failed. She still had not mastered that particular skill, but the memory of the golden-haired boy brought a smile to face. She turned to look at her mother.

"Mother, are you all right? You look even more tired than usual."

Katria smiled, "Today we present you to Crystal in the palace's chapel. After you are accepted, you will be presented to the people."

"Mother, what is the matter?"

"I'm sorry, Mar'ya, I will not be with you much longer. I have helped you all I can. The rest, I leave in the hands of Crystal and her Guardians. Be strong, My Child, and listen to the voice of Crystal. She will guide you. Come, let us go to the chapel."

Katria and Mar'ya stepped into the chapel that was the heart of the city. In the center of the room stood a huge, multifaceted crystal. Mar'ya dropped her mother's hand and approached the crystal alone. In her mind, she heard the soft weeping, the constant cry that had earned Crystal her title of 'The Weeping God'. In her heart she heard a whisper, *I love you.*

Mar'ya knelt before the large crystal, bowed her head, and whispered, "I am your true daughter. Guide me. My life is yours. Command me."

The crystal shimmered and a soft note drifted out the chapel and over the city, where the silent population waited. Mar'ya stood, turned away, and rejoined her mother. As Katria and Mar'ya stepped out on the balcony, a sigh drifted through the crowd. The young heir had been accepted. She carried the mark of Crystal: A silver streak in her midnight hair.

There was no wild cheering or celebration, however, for the people of Crystal knew that this young queen would have to fight the influence of the western lords, the greatest of whom was her father. There would be many dark days ahead. In all their hearts, silent prayers for her went to the mountains in the north.

Two days later, Mar'ya sat beside her mother, who was struggling to breathe. The illness that plagued her since childhood had grown worse. The days of the prophet had passed and the time of the heir was about to begin.

"Mar'ya, there is so much I want to say, and I have so little time left." Katria closed her eyes. "Where do I start? I love you. I am proud of you. Everything I have ever wanted in a daughter, I have found in you."

"Mother." Mar'ya did not hide her tears.

"Hush. Let me speak. Mar'ya, be careful who you trust," Katria paused, "Keep Mar and Kel close to you. They will love you and protect you. One will come out of the shadows, another from the desert, but the most important is Shen Oran Qualdar, Alana's son. Trust him."

"Shen is the western lord's lapdog. He disgraces the name of House Frya." Mar'ya snarled.

"Shen is not a warrior, but he will never betray you. There is wisdom in him. With your temper, you will need his tactful hand in dealing with the outsiders."

"Mother, I am only twelve. Who will stand for me until I am of age? My father?"

"Your father?" Katria laughed, then coughed. When she finally caught her breath, she continued, "NO! Do not let him near your throne. Do not give him or any western lord power in this city. If you do, you will lose everything. The Crystal Guardians will act for the land. They will train you to rule this land. However, they will not protect you. Your wits, your own inner strength, and your few true allies are all you have to depend on."

"Mother, I'm frightened. There is so much you still have not told me. So much. You must not die not now. What will I do without you?" Mar'ya wailed.

Katria sighed, "Mar'ya, you are very clever. I have faith in you. You must believe in yourself and remember the teachings of your Aunt

Alana. If you follow Crystal, she will help you make the right choices." Katria closed her eyes. Her voice was a whisper of sound when she continued, "Send my body to Crystal."

"Mother, wait. You can't leave me, not yet. Mother, please don't leave me. "

"Mar'ya there will be those who would gainsay you. They will try to have a western funeral for me. Swear that you will send me to Crystal"

"I swear. Mother, I love you, I love you so much." Mar'ya sobbed as Katria breathed her last.

Mar'ya opened the door of her room and nodded to the two House Mar guards standing outside, "Ring the crystal bells and send for the old women to prepare the queen's body." She commanded. One of the guards bowed his head, and left to do her bidding.

*****

"My mother will be sent to Crystal, as is the custom, at dawn tomorrow." Mar'ya made the announcement at the dinner table three hours later. "I have sent for the city women to prepare her body for the trip."

"My dear," her father smiled at her from the head of the table, "It was not necessary for you to do that. The wizards are here to take care of such things."

"It was Mother's final wish."

"Yes, well your mother has always been a little strange, and as her health deteriorated, she became even worse. Don't worry, I will take care of everything. By the way, Barak tells me you have been skipping your lessons."

Mar'ya shot a look of pure hatred at the wizard, "Sorry, I've been taking care of Mother."

"The wizards would have been happy to watch her for you." Her father smiled.

"I bet they would have." Mar'ya mumbled.

"Did you say something?" Her father asked. "This is why it's so important for you to not miss your classes. Young ladies should always speak clearly, that is, when they speak at all."

Mar'ya ignored him. She refused to get into an argument with her father, not now.

After an uncomfortable meal, Mar'ya returned to her mother's room, closely followed by Shen. Both of them missed the speculative look her father gave as they left.

"What do you want, Shen?" Mar'ya asked as they entered Katria's room.

"I am House Frya." Shen answered calmly.

"Oh, so you do remember who you are. I thought you were a new western lordling."

Shen ignored her comment, "Have you summoned the Crystal Guardians?"

"The bells have been sounded." She answered shortly, watching the women bathe and dress her mother's body. The women were weeping: Large tears ran down their cheeks as they tenderly wrapped Katria in a white shroud decorated with silver. "Silver, the tears of Crystal. No wonder there is so much silver in our mountains. Travel in peace, my mother," Mar'ya whispered. The ache in her heart threatened to tear her small body apart.

She hugged each of the women and whispered to them, "She loved you. I love you, thank you."

Shen watched Mar'ya with narrowed eyes. "Have you any idea how you will handle the storm tomorrow?"

"What storm?" Mar'ya asked blankly.

"Don't be stupid. Do you think there will be no arguments?"

"I rather hope there are. I am in a really foul mood."

Shen closed his eyes, "I will handle it."

"Shen, hear me; I am Mar'ya Olena. The Crystal Throne is mine, and any who stand between me and it, will die." Mar'ya wiped the tears off her cheeks with the back of her hand, and glared at Shen.

"Oh Crystal." Shen moaned, closed his eyes and stayed silent the rest of the night.

At dawn, the sound of the crystal bells echoed throughout the city as Mar'ya walked before the silent women carrying her mother's body downstairs. A group of wizards blocked her way.

Mar'ya glanced at the huge entrance doors to the castle, then back at the wizards standing between her and them.

"You are in my way."

"We will not allow this travesty to continue. Katria was a queen. She will be buried in the earth as befits her station. It is time for you people to give up your barbaric practices."

"Who are you?" Mar'ya frowned.

"I am Jarash, eldest of the wizards in Crystia."

"Then, Wizard Jarash, move. This is woman's business and none of yours."

"Women have no business. It is past time you and your Crystal Guardians realize that. Lord Richard is in charge now, and he demanded that his wife be buried in the western style."

Mar'ya took a deep breath, "Move." There was no trace of a grieving twelve-year-old in her voice. It was the voice of a queen and a goddess, cold and hard. "Hear me, man of the west, you and yours will be gone from my kingdom in twenty-four hours or you will die."

The wizard took an involuntary step backward. It was his turn to frown, "I will speak to your instructor. Barak has obviously failed in his training of you."

Shen stepped next to Mar'ya. He ignored the tension and announced "The Crystal Guardians are here."

"Open the doors." Mar'ya ordered, and two House Kel guards rushed to do her bidding.

The Crystal Guardians, twelve women, entered the room. Six of them stepped forward and took Katria's body, then turned and left the castle. The remaining six went straight to the chapel.

Mar'ya stepped around the wizards and headed toward the throne room. The guards, all wearing the colors of House Mar grinned at her and opened the door.

Her father looked up as she entered, "What are you doing here?" The mildness of his voice did not fool her.

"Where else would I be? This is my castle, my country, and my throne. By the way, if you sit in that chair, you will die." Mar'ya's voice was just as mild.

Richard raised an eyebrow, "Are you threatening me, Child?"

"No, it is written: 'Should a male sit upon the Crystal Throne, then shall he surely die'."

"You are a child. I, as your father, will act as your guardian until you are of age and safely married to one who will rule through you."

Mar'ya laughed. She had not meant to, but what her father said was ridiculous. Her father's face darkened, "Go to your room." He snarled.

Mar'ya ignored him and stepped up to the Crystal Throne on shaky legs. She did not sit, just stood in front of it and made her announcement.

"The Crystal Guardians are here. They will be acting as my guardians until they deem me worthy to rule. However, I still have the right to say who lives in my home. I want all these useless western noblemen to go back home. The wizards have already received their marching orders. Barak, if you agree to teach me magic, then I will allow you to stay. My father, of course, is welcome to stay or go. It matters not to me."

"Get this girl-child out of here." Richard trembled with fury.

Leon, Lord of Fishing House Wav, stepped forward and grabbed Mar'ya's arm.

"Take your hands off me." Mar'ya snarled. She grabbed the small eating knife out of her belt and slashed Lord Leon's arm. The man screamed and jerked his hand away.

"Guards, take this piece of carrion away and throw him in a cell until I get around to dealing with him."

"Shall we tend his wound?"

"Oh no. After all only a girl-child cut him. I'm sure a big, strong male like him won't suffer too much." Mar'ya simpered, staring absently at the blood on her dress. "Oh dear, the fool has ruined my new dress."

The guards grinned as they took Leon away.

Mar'ya waited until they were gone, then smiled at all those in the room. "Well, that seems to conclude the business of the day. You are all dismissed. Quite a few of you do have some packing to do, I will see you all off tomorrow."

She watched the men file silently out of the room then turned to her father. "I am, after all, your daughter. Did you think I would allow you to run roughshod over me?"

Richard looked at her and smiled nastily "I wonder." He breathed quietly.

Mar'ya missed his soft reply as she left the room, both her stomach and her mind in turmoil.

Oh Crystal, I'm going to be sick. My legs are shaking, my hands are sweating, and I just attacked one of the House Lords. My father is going to kill me. Why do I lose my temper? Why can't I learn to pick my battles more wisely? I am tired and frightened. Crystal guide and guard me.

*****

Two weeks later, Mar'ya stood in the council chamber, exhausted from fighting with her stubborn House Lords. She refused to allow her father to rule Cristia in her name. Today, the Crystal Guardians finally made their presence known, and now there was a grudging and fragile working relationship growing between the House Lords, the Crystal Guardians, and Mar'ya.

"Your Highness, I am Anton, House Wav. What has become of House Lord Leon?"

Mar'ya stared blankly at the man for a moment then shrugged, "I forgot all about him. Guards, bring Leon to the chambers."

A shocked gasp ran through the onlookers as Lord Leon stumbled into the room.

Mar'ya studied him for a moment, "I had to get a new eating knife. Your house will be charged." She smiled. "Unfortunately, Lord Leon's arm became septic and had to be removed. Let this be a reminder to all of you, I will be Crystal Queen, and any who lays hand on my person shall suffer the same fate. Hear me."

"We hear thee." The council members repeated in shock.

Mar'ya smiled, nodded, and left the House Lords to the tender mercies of the Crystal Guardians.

Chapter Four

Mar'ya scowled. It was her sixteenth birthday, and her father was forcing her to go through the demeaning ritual that was instituted during her grandmother's time.

"Mar'ya, did you hear me?"

"Why, Father, I did not realize you even knew my name." She said flippantly.

"I am serious, Girl, you go through the ceremony with a candidate of my choice and I will leave this backwards, godforsaken country to you."

"Why?"

"Because I am tired of trying to civilize you; tired of fighting your people and these creatures calling themselves Crystal Guardians. Barak will stay and give you the limited training you are capable of." He smiled nastily, "It seems that you are not the powerful witch your mother hoped for."

Mar'ya shrugged, "I want it in writing."

"You don't trust me? Unnatural child, to say such a thing to your loving father who has only your best interests at heart."

"Write!"

Laughing, her father wrote their agreement and signed it. "I will leave first thing in the morning."

Mar'ya took the paper from him and returned to her rooms. This was not turning out to be a good day. The Crystal Guardians announced that they would oversee her kingdom for two more years. Barak told her that his testing showed she had only minimal power, but he added he would continue to work with her, and in another ten years or so, he would test her again, "Some people," he said smugly, "Improve with training, but not very much."

Now she had to share her body with some male of her father's choosing. *Damn. There has to be some way I can get out of this. Instead of losing my temper, now is the time for me to use my mind and try to come up with a plan.*

A tentative knock on the door broke into her thoughts. *Oh Crystal, time's up.*

She opened the door to find Shen looking very uncomfortable, standing outside.

"What are you doing here?"

"Umm your father sent me?"

"You? Oh come in. Stop standing outside the door like an idiot," Mar'ya slammed the door shut, then turned to face her cousin. "I hope you don't expect me to go through with this."

"You would have had to, if he had sent anyone else," Shen's voice was mild.

"No. I have a plan." Mar'ya said smugly.

Shen raised his eyebrows, "You? Have a plan? Do share."

"Stop being sarcastic, Shen. Okay, here's the deal: You spend the night in my rooms, we let everyone think whatever they want, and when I take control of the Crystal Throne you become my chief advisor."

Shen nodded, "That's good. Who came up with that?"

"Shen!"

Shen grinned, walked over to her bed and stretched out on it. "I'm thinking. Let's see, Lord Leon lost an arm for laying his hands on you. Umm, let us not consider the painful loss I could suffer. On the other hand, there is the promise of future power; I mean, your chief advisor has a lot of clout."

"Shen, get off my bed." She sat next to him. "I'm serious, I really don't want to do this."

"Oh, you wound me. Don't you find me attractive?"

"Shen, it has nothing to do with you. I don't want anyone. Anyway, I remember when you were a runny-nosed, dirty faced brat."

"Actually you don't. I was past that point when you showed up." Shen sat up, studied her face for a moment, and nodded. "Okay."

"Huh?"

"I said okay. I hope you realize that your father will want proof."

"What?"

"Oh Crystal." Shen sighed, "Lay down and hand me your knife."

"Shen, what are you doing?"

"Relax, this won't hurt much." He grinned as he pushed her skirt up and made a shallow cut on the inside of her leg.

"Nice legs."

"Ouch! Shen, you maniac, that hurt."

"Ooh good, very good. That should convince anyone listening outside. Now shut up and go to sleep."

The next morning, she and Shen went downstairs. Her father stared at her, then went past her and into her room. A few moments later, he came out, a smile on his face. "If I didn't know better I would have thought you two were more closely related than just cousins." He nodded at the startled look on Shen's face as he walked out of the Crystal Palace, never to return.

"Shen, what was that all about?"

Shen shrugged, "How would I know?"

"Well, Chief Advisor, what do we do now?"

"Let's go talk to the Crystal Guardians. You still have two more years until they leave, take advantage of it. Work with them and learn the things you need to know so that you can govern wisely."

"Good idea." She paused, "Umm, Shen, I didn't hurt your feelings did I?"

"Crystal, no! I got the best part of the deal. I was worried how I was going to talk you out of asking me to, ahh, perform my duty."

"OH! Oh, sorry, I mean, I didn't want to embarrass you. I mean, it doesn't matter, you are still my favorite cousin. I mean, it does not matter who you like." Mar'ya blushed.

Shen stared at her blankly, then closed his eyes, "Oh Crystal," he rubbed the bridge of his nose, "Anyway, I think we will be able to work well together." He said at last.

"Yeah, me too." Mar'ya replied cheerfully.

*****

Richard, Emperor of the West, returned home after his long years in the east. He looked at his city as he passed through and nodded. "The priests and the wizards have done well, I will have to compliment them on their care of my city." He stretched his long legs out.

"Thank your son, Lord Gregor, not the priests or the wizards." The other man in the carriage with him snarled.

"Problems, Lord Glenn of Arnus?" Richard glanced at the father of his first wife.

"The boy is my grandson, and I love him. I am proud of him, but the price he paid to keep your people safe and healthy is not one any child should have to bear."

"Explain yourself," mild annoyance colored Richard's voice.

"Oh, he's free now. He's too old to play bitch to that soft, slimy Wizard Imalee, but when he was younger…" The old man took a deep breath, "I should have killed that child lover when I first suspected."

"My son," Richard frowned, "Imalee dared touch my son?"

"Well who was going to stop him? I am a very minor lord. Only your taking my daughter as first wife gave me any status. Besides, Imalee is a wizard. No one may question them. You weren't here to protect the boy, and none of us know what damage the boy has suffered."

"I was doing the will of our god." Richard protested.

"Well then, any decent god would have protected his next emperor while you were off enjoying doing his will." Lord Glenn snarled.

"Is that what the people think, that I was enjoying myself?" Richard smiled bitterly. "I longed for my home and civilized companions every moment I was away."

"For twenty years, my Emperor? If you say so, but is power that important to you?"

"Not for me, but my son will rule the entire world. That is what I labored in exile for twenty years to accomplish." Richard objected.

Lord Glenn smiled bitterly, "Don't expect him or the people to understand or forgive you. Me, when the welcome party is over, I will be leaving your capitol and your stinking wizards. They are not welcome in Arnus, nor are you."

"That is treason." Richard spoke mildly.

"Then chop off my head. I am an old man, do you think I care?" Lord Glenn closed his eyes and lay back in his seat.

Richard stepped out of the carriage and studied those gathered on the steps to greet him; his first wife, Merle, in her veils stood next to a tall, broad-shouldered, young man. Behind them stood the leaders of the Wizard Council and the high priests. Richard frowned, "Where is the boy's first wife?" He asked his father-in-law.

"He doesn't have one. He spends all his time with the army. He's a good leader, and the troops will follow him anywhere." Lord Glenn climbed out of the coach, "Now, if you'll excuse me, my Lord Emperor, I must go and prepare my family to leave this cesspool you call home."

Richard sighed, then he saw Imalee standing next to Jarash, and his eyes hardened. With long strides, he mounted the steps and nodded to Merle "Gregor, my wizard council, I will see you in my chambers. Now." He snapped as he walked past the group.

Merle's dark eyes snapped with malice as she glanced at Imalee on her way to her rooms. The wizard shrugged, a slight smile on his face.

A few minutes later, the last of the wizards entered the room where Richard waited. "My Lord, that was not well done. We are not yours to command. We serve Storm's will. Do not order us around as if we were slaves in your palace." Bunji, leader of the Wizard Council scolded.

"Bunji, be silent! You and your useless parasites live at my pleasure. If you truly wish to serve your god, then go into the wilderness where he is supposed to live and stay there."

"Richard, you dare to speak that way to us? You have lived too long with the barbarians of the east. You have forgotten what is acceptable in civilized lands. Without us, you would have no empire." Bunji raised his hand.

"That is Lord Emperor Richard, to you, Bunji." Richard shook his head, "Try to cast that spell, and you will die." He added and smiled at the stunned look on the faces around him. "You are quite right. I have spent too much time in the east, but what you don't know is that once you left, your control over me went away. Barak was not strong enough to keep the mind lock you had established going." Richard glanced at his son, "Do you suffer a lot of headaches?" He asked, then smiled grimly at the startled look on the younger man's face, "Yes, that is how they control us, stop us from thinking, and force us to do their will. If you decide to fight it, you can. Don't let the pain deter you, for once the lock is broken, they cannot reestablish it."

Richard stepped up to Imalee, reached out and grabbed the wizard around his throat. "You stink of corruption and filth. You are not fit to represent our god. More importantly, you have abused your power, and hurt my son. The penalty for treason against the emperor and our god is death." Richard's voice was mild as he snapped Imalee's neck. He walked over to the door, opened it and beckoned to the guards outside, "Take this body and burn it publicly. Let all know that the justice of the emperor and Storm is swift and final."

After Imalee's body had been dragged from the room, Richard turned to Bunji, "Well, Wizard, do you have anything to say?"

Bunji scowled, "Imalee may have deserved what happened, but it was not your place to judge him. Be careful, Emperor, you have crossed the bounds of what is acceptable."

Richard studied the wizard for a long, tense moment then turned to his son, "You are my heir. I hear you have done well by the people. I am proud of you."

"So, I am supposed to fall on my knees in gratitude? What you have done is too late. While you were cavorting with the whores in Crystia, your people suffered. Now, you walk in and expect us to welcome you as our savior? Where were you when we needed you? Was your new family more important to you than us?" Gregor asked angrily.

"I have opened the door for you to rule the east. The whole world will be yours to command. Storm has promised me this." Richard explained.

"I don't want the world. I can barely rule the lands under my control as it is. Why should I desire to rule some barbaric country that will consume even more of our resources to educate and civilize?" The young man demanded.

"You could always send the entire Wizard Council to do the job for you." Richard said slyly, and smiled at the thoughtful look on his son's face.

Richard turned and walked out of the room, leaving a thoughtful Gregor and an angry Wizard Council staring after him.

Three months later, the western empire mourned the loss of their emperor. According to the wizards, Richard died of a strange, wasting disease contracted in the east. Merle returned to her father's estates, and Gregor was crowned the twenty-seventh emperor of the West.

Chapter Five

The man was beautiful: Black hair; emerald eyes; broad shoulders; long, muscular legs; firm buns; and a smile to die for. The dusting of sliver at his temples made him even more attractive. Mar'ya watched him walk across the foyer of the castle and talk to one of the guards. "Crystal, he moves like a cat." She whispered.

"Stop drooling. It is not becoming of a queen." Shen elbowed her sharply.

"Shen, who is he?" Mar'ya still stared at the newcomer.

"I am jealous, heartbroken. I can't believe you would throw me over for a pretty face."

Mar'ya smiled dreamily, "And long legs, and…"

"Crystal, I'm going to be sick." Shen interrupted.

"Shen, do you know who he is?"

"Yes. So do you." Shen had a smug look on his face.

"No, I do not. Now are you going to introduce us?"

"As soon as you wipe your mouth." Shen smirked, then added with a malicious grin, "You really don't recognize him?"

"Shen, you are being mean."

"Yep."

"Oh Crystal," Mar'ya breathed, "He's coming towards us."

"So this our new queen? She grew up well." The man's voice was deep, and smooth.

"Butter cream," Mar'ya said softly. Then blushed as both men turned to stare at her.

"Butter cream, I smell the cakes." Mar'ya said quickly.

"Ahh," the newcomer smiled, "Our queen is thinking of her stomach."

"A little lower than that, I'd say." Shen grinned.

"Shen! It's my eighteenth birthday, be nice to me." Mar'ya wailed.

Shen smiled, "My queen, may I present the Merchant Lord, and your cousin, Alex Sultav. His mate is Crystal Guardian Solari. Now do you remember him?"

Mar'ya looked closely at Alex, "You got older." She blurted, then blushed as the memory of a crossed eyed young face with golden hair flashed into her mind.

"Happy birthday, Your Majesty. It is my pleasure to meet you again. My wife has told me a lot about you." Alex graciously ignored her remark.

"I bet." Mar'ya grumbled

"All good things: You are stubborn, headstrong, and a true daughter of Crystal. I look forward to working with you." Alex bowed.

"To working with me?"

"Shen, didn't you tell Mar'ya about me?"

Shen grabbed a sandwich off one of the tables, took a bite, and shook his head, "I forgot. Anyway, she should be able to figure out who you are without my help."

Alex, removed the half eaten sandwich from Shen's fingers, "Don't talk with your mouth full." He chided gently, then finished the sandwich.

Mar'ya stared at both of them, and swallowed the giggle that rose into her throat. "Ahem, let's see. Sultav, so you are a cousin, but which of the Merchant Houses are you lord of?"

"I told you, he is a cousin. You never heard of his House because he doesn't have one." Shen frowned. "All right, listen up, this is Alex Sultav, a Merchant Lord, and a cousin. He's a bit of a dandy and no one takes him seriously, mainly because he is a merchant with no ships, and no shop. We put up with him because his wife is the senior-named Crystal Guardian."

Mar'ya glanced around the crowded room, and nodded. "And he's cute," she smiled. "Those were good days," She whispered as she walked away.

"So, what do we have?" Alex asked Shen as the two men watched her retreating figure.

"A handful." Shen said with a sigh, and moved off in the opposite direction.

Mar'ya lost sight of both men during the celebration. Later, Crystal Guardian Solari approached her.

"Happy birthday, Your Highness."

"Thank you, Crystal Guardian Solari." Mar'ya grabbed the last slice of her birthday cake off the table.

"I saw you talking to my husband earlier. Is this the first time you met him since you grew up?" Solari smiled.

"Yes. I remember Gail saying he was cute, but now that I'm older, I realize he is absolutely delicious. Where did you find him?" Mar'ya asked.

Solari laughed, "Yes he is. He is also your mother's first cousin." She ignored the last part of Mar'ya's question.

"How did my mother let him get away from her?"

"Oh, I saw him first, and your mother's eyes were always in the mountains." Solari paused, "Anyway, I came over to congratulate you, and to let you know that the Guardians are all very proud of you. You have the potential to become one of Crystia's greatest rulers."

Mar'ya's eyes widened, "Really?" she breathed.

"Yes, really. Don't let that go to your head, however. Keep caring for your people, and trying to do what is best for them. You'll do just fine." Solari glanced around, "Well, most of your guests have left and it's time for me to leave as well. Good night, Mar'ya."

Shen joined Mar'ya as she started up the stairs to her rooms. "That went rather well."

"Where were you all night Shen?" Mar'ya glanced at him.

"Around." Shen grinned, "I saw you talking to Solari earlier."

"Yes. I have always liked her. Shen, I wish that there were more women among my House Lords."

"Lonely?" Shen asked sympathetically.

"Uh huh."

Shen tugged Mar'ya's hair and smiled, "In the old days, there were female House Lords, but that changed about two hundred years ago."

"Why? What happened?"

"We really don't know, but House Frya suspects that the wizard council had something to do with it."

Mar'ya grinned, "According to Barak, House Frya is paranoid. He says that the wizard council has more important things to do than try to manipulate every little country they go to. He says it's not their fault that societies change once the people are educated."

Shen frowned, "Do you believe him?" From the corner of his eye, he saw Alex following them.

"I don't know. I think the truth lies somewhere in between."

"You threw the wizard council out of the country." Shen reminded her.

"Well, I was young and angry at the time."

"So you would let them back if they asked?" Shen pressed.

"Shen, they did some good things. They trained the people in magic, and they are good healers."

"Really? Who did they train? Show me two of our witches that they trained."

Mar'ya shrugged, "I don't want to talk about that now."

Shen reached around her and opened the door to her rooms, "Well, go on in. It's time you met your other advisor."

Shen pushed her gently into her room as he and Alex entered behind her.

"Alex? What are you doing here?"

"Mar'ya, Alex will tell you what is going on in your country. He has no House affiliations, and no reason to lie to you. His only loyalty is to Crystal and the throne. Nothing happens in Crystia or the Stoneland Desert that Alex does not know about." Shen said as he closed the door.

Alex stretched, "Thanks for the glowing recommendation, Shen, but I'm not quite that good. Almost, but not quite. Cousin, I am your spy; your ears and your eyes. I worked for your mother. If you wish, I will continue doing the same job for you."

"Why do I need a spy?" Mar'ya asked. "Our country has no enemies."

Alex glanced at Shen, "How much of our history does she know?"

Shen shook his head. "Barak has been filling her ears with his stories and she believes him." Shen said flatly.

"Sit!" Alex commanded.

Mar'ya sat, "Alex Sultav, don't you ever speak to me in that tone of voice again."

"Cousin, I know you are not an idiot, so just be very still and listen to what I tell you. Listen and believe. Do not interrupt. Hush!" He snapped when Mar'ya opened her mouth to object.

"One thousand and five hundred years ago, something happened to the four gods of this world. Only the Mistresses of House Frya know what it was, and not even they know whose fault it was. We mortals call it the beginning of the grieving. About five hundred years later, the wizards showed up. In the beginning, all they did was aggravate the already tense situation between the city and the nomads. They did not interfere with our politics or the way our Houses were governed."

"I know all that, they have never interfered…"

"Wrong!" Alex interrupted her. "Five hundred years ago, they started spouting their nonsense about women not being fit to rule. There were wizards in every major House. They didn't bother with the smaller Houses, they still don't. About fifty years later there were no women House Lords in any major House in Crystia. Then, about a hundred years later they began training any girl child of power in those Houses, usurping House Frya's authority. Not long afterwards, oh, about two generations, the birth rate of witches started to decline.

"For a while, only the smaller Houses to the east produced any witches at all. The power of the Throne Holders remained strong, for the heir was always sent to Frya for training. Then your great-grandmother broke the cycle. Belia, your grandmother, was trained by the wizards, and she was a total disaster as Throne Holder. The only good thing she did was marry a man from House Frya. He took your mother home with him to meet his family. Belia was so entranced by the westerners, that she did not object. She already had a plan to place a western lord on the Crystal Throne. Unfortunately, your mother was not physically strong, but her power to see the future; led her to place her life at risk so that you could be born. She foresaw that you would have the opportunity to bring back the old ways and reverse the decline of the witches."

"You only have circumstantial evidence against the wizards." Mar'ya cried.

Alex shook his head, "How many of your House Lords do you trust?"

Mar'ya frowned, "I never thought about it; Mar, Kel, Frya, Sua, and maybe Orin."

"All of them are small Houses from the eastern part of Crystia. None of them have any dealing with wizards. The large Houses. Where are their daughters? Why are they never brought to the city? You have no female attendants from any of your major Houses," Alex paused, "Do you have any female attendants?"

Mar'ya shook her head slowly, "There is Mase."

Alex clenched his fists, "Mase should have been a witch and House Lord Sa. Her mother brought her to the castle to serve the Throne. The wizards and the western lords put their hands on her, treated her the way they did their western women, and Belia did nothing to protect the child. Her brother, Gerad, who is now House Lord Sa, hates the wizards and all they stand for. He will not trade with the westerners or even speak with them. That is why you have no female attendants from the smaller Houses. They no longer trust the Throne to protect their daughters. You have to prove yourself to gain their complete trust."

Mar'ya bowed her head, "I did not know." She whispered.

Alex stared at her, "Leave your perfumed, western wizard in the castle; take Shen and your guards. Go among your people. Speak with them, hear what they have to tell you. That is the only truth you need to hear: The only truth that matters. You are their leader, your job is to protect them." He opened the door, "When you decide whose queen you are, let me know." He whispered closing the door behind him.

*****

"So, cousin, how do you feel after a year of walking the streets of your city and visiting the smaller Houses?" Shen threw himself down on Mar'ya's bed.

"Get off my bed," she said mildly. With a sigh she walked to her window, "Shen, not one of the larger Houses wanted me to visit. There was always an excuse or a reason why I could not come to visit. The people in the city and the smaller Houses; they are terrified of the wizards and the westerners. I did not realize how much harm those groups had done to my people. Why didn't you tell me?"

"Would have you believed me?" Shen sat up.

"Yes. No, I don't know."

"Exactly. So can you answer Alex's question?"

"Oh yes," Mar'ya turned from the window, "I am Crystia's Queen. I will protect my people no matter what it costs me. I will depend on you and Alex to keep me current on the western empire's latest maneuvers, and how best to keep Crystia safe.

"I didn't realize that being queen would take so much work." Mar'ya sat on a chair, then frowned. "Excuse me, what is wrong with this picture?"

"Just being queen is not hard work. Being a good queen, however, is another story." Shen grinned, "What picture?"

"Oh, never mind. Get off my bed and go find something useful to do."

Chapter Six

"Mase, quit fussing with my hair. Just tie it back."

"But Highness, it's your birthday. You should do something special."

"Mase, you have been with me for fourteen years and I love you dearly, but I have many things on my mind today. I promise to let you primp me all you wish for dinner. Now, however, I have a meeting with my council of House Leaders, so will you please hurry up." Mar'ya tried to keep the annoyance out of her voice.

"Highness, all the House Lords will be there. Don't you want to look pretty for them?"

The older woman, who had taken the place of Mar'ya's mother, put her hands on her ample hips, and glared at Mar'ya. "It is way past the time for you to start a family. You are twenty-four and have chosen no one. The people are worried about the future of the Crystal Throne. Who will lead us if you leave no heirs?"

"The people of Crystal have every right to worry about the future, but there are more pressing dangers facing us than my starting a family."

"This is not right. A pretty, young woman like you should have a nice husband to share all these problems with." Mase muttered.

Mar'ya grinned, "I have Shen, and Alex."

"A young, Frya pretty-boy, and a Merchant with no house name. Fine selections for a queen."

"I can trust them." Mar'ya answered shortly. "Now, I have to leave. We will not continue this conversation again."

Mase snorted, "Don't try that queen speech with me. I am a woman of Crystal, and have the right to say anything I want."

Mar'ya stared at Mase for a moment then laughed, "Yes, you are, and yes, you do." She hugged the older woman and walked into her sitting room, where Shen waited for her.

"Shen. I greet thee."

Shen frowned, "Why so formal all of a sudden?"

"I am waiting for your lecture."

"What lecture? Oh, by the way, happy birthday."

"That's it, just happy birthday?"

"Okay, you obviously have something to say. Go ahead. Get it out."

Mar'ya sighed, "I have just received a lecture from Mase about my duty to produce future generations of Throne Holders." She looked around the room, "Where is Alex?"

Shen grinned, "Thinking about talking the shadow advisor into taking the job?"

"Oh Crystal, no. He is way too old. Besides he has a perfectly good wife, who also happens to be a Crystal Guardian."

"I'll pass that message on." Shen laughed and dodged the cushion his queen threw at him."

"Shen, am I mistaken, or are there even more Mar and Kel guards around the castle than usual." Mar'ya glanced at the four guards accompanying them to the council chamber.

"No and yes. Mar'ya, do you remember all the houses the western lords built while they were in the city?"

"Yes, the whole western district. According to Grandmother, it was fitting. What about it?"

"Would you mind if Alex and I loaned those properties to some of our people?"

"Mar and Kel?"

"Yes, also some of the farming houses. There are a lot of empty warehouses in that area."

"Are things really that bad?"

"Alex seems to think so."

"Do you have a list?"

"Right here." Shen handed her a small roll of parchment.

Mar'ya scanned the list quickly, then nodded. "I'll just give the palaces outright to the selected families."

*****

The House Lords all stood as Mar'ya and Shen entered the council room. Mar'ya sat at the head of the table and nodded her permission for the others to sit.

Leon of Wav, the one armed House Lord bowed his head, "On behalf of the Crystal House Lords, I wish you a happy twenty-fourth birthday, Your Highness."

"My thanks to the Crystal House Lords for their well wishing." Mar'ya answered formally, as she waited for the rest of what she knew was about to be said.

Leon cleared his throat, "In accordance with custom, your House Lords have created a short list of prospective consorts for your consideration."

"What custom would that be, House Wav?" Mar'ya interrupted him. "Custom decrees the Crystal Guardians make that decision."

"Your grandmother…"

"My grandmother ignored custom and forced my mother to wed a man who already had a wife and children."

"Their customs are different from ours. In the west, there is no wrong in a leader having more that one wife."

Mar'ya smiled, "Then that means I may have more than one husband?" she asked softly.

"Your Highness, a man may do this thing. A woman needs behave more modestly."

"Wav, shut up and sit down before I have your tongue removed." Mar'ya glared at the old man and noted, not for the first time, the hatred in his eyes as he glared back at her.

"Give me your list, I will have the Crystal Guardians go over it."

"And you will hold to their decision?"

"I will consider it."

"Is there any pressing business we need to discuss at this time?" Mar'ya waited a heartbeat then continued. "Good. I will see you all at dinner."

She stood and headed for the door, then stopped. "By the way, I have not yet received the annual reports from the following houses: Tau, Sa, Capra, Mar, Kel, Sua, Orin, Agon, Trata and Paron." Mar'ya frowned, "Look, why don't you all just bring the paperwork to my office in an hour, then we will have the rest of the day to celebrate."

Shen closed the door behind them and followed his headstrong queen to her offices.

"You have angered the House Lords." Shen said mildly.

"All of them?"

"Yes. Your inference that certain Houses were lax in reporting their income to you embarrassed those who would be your allies."

"A little embarrassment does not hurt anyone."

"Mar'ya, threatening to remove Wav's tongue did not win you any friends, nor did your statement about taking two husbands."

Mar'ya laughed, "Shen, you are much too serious. Leon of Wav hates me. He always has, he always will."

"And the two husbands?"

"Oh, well now, that is another matter. I will give it my most serious consideration."

Shen dropped his head and sighed, "Oh Crystal, I feel a headache coming on."

"Actually, the young queen has done better than I expected." A thread of laughter wove through the new voice.

"Alex, when did you get back?" Mar'ya walked over and hugged her cousin.

"Never left."

"Alex."

Alex sighed, "Mar'ya, I am House Shadow. You know; creep, sneak, eavesdrop, all the good, fun stuff."

Mar'ya laughed, "Where's my birthday present?"

Alex looked at her in mock surprise, then fell to his knees before her "I forgot. Oh, my most gracious queen, can you find it in your compassionate heart to forgive me?"

"No! Off with his head."

"Err, shouldn't that be off with his arm, or maybe out with his tongue?" Alex stood up and laughed.

"Alex, for Crystal's sake, do not encourage her." Shen protested glaring at both his cousins.

"Relax, Shen." Alex laughed.

"Oh Crystal, the Sultav madness has struck again." Shen groaned.

Alex patted Shen on the back and Mar'ya stuck her tongue out at him. She sighed, the gaiety of the moment gone, "So what is going on?"

Alex threw himself carelessly into a chair. His dark eyes were grim, "The last merchant ship to the west has still not returned."

Shen shook his head, "I spoke to the ambassador. That snake oil salesman merely extolled the dangers of sea travel and the bravery of men who dare to sail. However, he did hint that if you should decide to become a vassal state of the western empire and return all properties stolen from western lords, the empire would assist in the search for our people."

"Shen, continue dealing with him. Stall, but give him the impression that, if, as a gesture of good faith, the ship was returned, I would do whatever he asked. Afterwards, we can send him back to his masters."

"You would have me lie?"

"I would have you lie, cheat, steal; whatever is necessary to get our people home."

"That means war." Shen warned.

"Shen, I do not intend to hand my kingdom over to the western empire. However, we need time; time to sort out the traitors and get most of our people to safety."

"We cannot defeat the empire alone." Alex leaned forward in his chair. "So what are you planning?"

"We are not alone. We are not the only ones who would be threatened if the empire invades the east. We are not the only nation on this continent."

"The nomads?" Alex asked, watching her closely.

"No!" Shen objected.

"Why not?" Alex shifted his attention to Shen. "A real reason, Shen: Not ancient prejudices fostered by the wizards, but a reason that has fact behind it. Do you know any of the nomads?"

Shen shook his head, "No."

Mar'ya studied both men, "Shen, you deal with the ambassador. Will you do that?"

Before Shen could answer her, the sound of bells announced the approach of the Crystal Guardians. The door opened and an old woman walked into the room.

"Shen, House Frya, the only male who will ever become a Named Guardian; Mar'ya, Throne Holder, has chosen wisely. The prophecy now moves toward its fulfillment. Obey her or House Frya will close its eyes to you and the future will be ashes. Alex of the Shadows, go to the desert and speak these words to them; 'For behold, storms come that will break the rocks and blow away all mists. The blooming of the desert moves upon us with great speed. Gather your warriors so that the will of the gods may come to pass.'

"Mar'ya, true daughter of Crystal, and Witch of the Crystal Throne, the days of testing are upon you, and on your strength of will rests the survival of eastern lands. I am the eldest of the Nameless Crystal Guardians, and I have spoken the words of Crystal."

Mar'ya, Shen and Alex bowed their heads and completed the ancient ritual of obedience, "The Nameless Crystal Guardian has spoken. We have heard the words of Crystal and we will obey."

The old woman nodded. "Mar'ya, you dream true. Follow your dreams." She turned and left the room.

Alex stood up and stretched, "Well, I have my assignment, so I'll be on my way."

"Alex, be careful. If I lost you or Shen, I would have no strength left to fight."

Alex ruffled his young cousin's hair, "Mar'ya, Witch of the Crystal, and my Queen, you will hold strong. I believe in you." He smiled, "See you in three months." Then he, too, was gone.

"Shen?"

"It's okay, Mar'ya, I will never betray you. Only death would make me leave your side."

Shen looked at her as the import of the Guardian's words registered, "Mar'ya, I'm going to be a Crystal Guardian, I'll be the first male ever."

"Shen," Mar'ya smiled gently, "Only if our nation survives, will that come to pass, so let us both work hard to make sure it happens." She stretched and yawned, "Oh Crystal, I'm starving. Is it lunchtime yet?"

Shen grinned, "In about an hour. You have another set of meetings to sit through, remember?"

"Yeah, well have lunch served in here for everyone." She looked around, "Think we have enough space for that?"

"Twelve people will fit, any more, though, and we will be in trouble. Mar'ya, aren't you at all curious about the message the Crystal Guardians gave to Alex?"

Mar'ya waited until Shen passed her orders on to the guard outside the door and returned to his seat before she answered him.

"Do you know what it meant?"

"No."

"Well, I guess the nomads have their own version of the Crystal Guardians, and they will understand. No one ever knows what the Crystal Guardians are talking about anyway. They love riddles. I hate riddles."

Shen grinned, "No patience."

"Nope." Mar'ya smiled back.

Five minutes later, twelve angry House Lords stormed into the office, all of them talking at once. Mar'ya sat quietly behind her desk, watching them. She grinned and rang the small bell on her desk.

"I love you." She announced in the silence.

"Damn funny way of showing it." One of the older men grumbled.

"I love you all so much that I don't think I could survive unless you all were in the city with me."

The Lords glanced at each other, then sat down warily. "So this is not about annual reports?" one asked.

Mar'ya shook her head. "Do you love me?"

"Your Highness, I am Van, Merchant House Lord Agon. You are our queen. We know that all you do is for the good of the land. You bring back the old ways, and you care for your people. We love you. Lead us and we will follow."

Mar'ya looked around the room. The other House Lords nodded their heads in agreement.

"So then, let us move on to annual reports. Sa and Capra how is the fishing?"

"Very good. We could bring in record catches every week if we wanted."

Mar'ya nodded, "You want. Smoke, salt and dry the extra. Keep accurate count and store it in your new warehouse in the western district. Know any smugglers gentlemen?"

"Your Highness, would we cheat the throne of its honest revenues?" Carol, House Lord Capra, smiled.

"Well then, find some. By the end of the season, I want every ship hidden. Also, find out if those smugglers and thieves that do not exist know of hidden ways into the city. Learn them. There are palaces in the western district large enough to hold a small house, pick one that suits your needs. Move your people in and let Shen know. He will make sure you have a legal deed for the property."

"Orin and Tau how are the crops shaping up?"

"Well, Highness, we had a bit of trouble in our area, so there's not as much as we expected, but we do have high hopes for the second crop." Pat, House Lord Orin replied.

"Rain?" She asked mildly.

Both House Lords squirmed.

"Gentleman and Lady?" Mar'ya encouraged.

"Well, Highness, it's not much known, but a lot of our people have taken mates from among the nomads."

"No! Really?" Mar'ya shook her head, "So what does this aberrant behavior on your part have to do with the crops?"

"Highness." There was a warning in Shen's voice.

Mar'ya smiled, "Shen, hush. They know I love them, and I do believe that House Lord Pat's mother was a Sultav."

Pat smiled, "House Orin apologizes to the Crown. What I should have said was some of our in-laws had small crop problems, so we loaned them a bit of food."

"They will repay the loan?"

"Yes, Highness, second crop looks good all around."

"Choose a warehouse, store the crops, and try to get as much as you can. We may have another harvest, but don't bet on it."

"I suppose you want our Houses in the city as well?"

"At the end of the last harvest. Is that going to be a problem?"

"No, Your Highness. If we could get a bit of land in the city, we could send some of the older folk in early and start small gardens."

"Use the park. The two of you work it out. By the way, are the nomads starving?"

"Oh no, Highness," Pat glanced at Tau House Lord Rik, "We do a bit of trading, you see, just for House use."

"Taxes?" Mar'ya raised an eyebrow.

"Well, I mean, it's just a little. Nothing worth mentioning. It's not really trading, just some cousins will bring dates or figs, and we give grain. You know, family."

Mar'ya nodded, "Let Shen know what you need. Don't move in for the next three months."

"House Sua?"

"Yes. Your Highness, capture, kill, smoke, salt, choose warehouse, choose house, move in."

"House Lord Evan, you are magnificent." Mar'ya cooed.

"Tell my wife." Evan scowled, and the others in the room chuckled.

"By the way, people, this is a secret. No House not present is to be told about our plans. Houses Mar and Kel, you will be responsible for security in both the western district and the palace. If you need extra manpower, recruit some of the merchant seamen. I hear they are very good at splitting heads."

"We going to be splitting heads soon?" Evan's face broke into a toothless grin.

"House Lord Evan, the answer to that is probably sooner than we expect."

"Not going to split any nomad's head." Evan frowned.

"No, we are not splitting nomad's heads. Evan, stop speaking that way. I know you can speak properly, I heard your speech in council a few weeks ago and you were absolutely brilliant."

Evan grinned, "I love you."

Mar'ya glanced at the ceiling and groaned just as the door opened and the servants delivered lunch.

Chapter Seven

"The empire's ambassador is here to see you, Your Highness." Shen announced.

Mar'ya frowned, "Has our ship been returned?"

"It arrived this morning with an escort of two empire warships. Our people are being examined by the Named Crystal Guardians now. Oh, and the empire's warships are still standing off shore at the river's mouth."

"Thank goodness our river is too shallow for them to get near the city. Have you heard from Alex?"

"He is on his way home. According to him the message was received and understood, whatever that means."

"Some days he is as bad as the Crystal Guardians. Oh well, here goes nothing. Send the ambassador in, Shen, and please remain in the room."

Mar'ya finished signing the papers before her, then glanced up at High Lord Mervin Sonne, Ambassador of the Western Empire to Crystia.

"Please, Lord Sonne, be seated. I am sorry to have kept you waiting, but you did arrive earlier than expected."

Lord Sonne smiled, "No, no quite all right, I'm just pleased that we could solve all our little problems so easily."

Mar'ya blinked, "Which little problems, my Lord?"

"Well, now that you have become a vassal state to the empire, my Lord Emperor Gregor is taking his responsibility as your older brother very seriously. Your future husband and his staff of twelve wizards are on the ship, awaiting the permission of your House Lords to come ashore."

Lord Sonne leaned forward, "You are very lucky. Your new husband, Lord Michael Prevor, is the most sought after of our young lords. He is from a very influential family. You will, of course, be first wife as befits the sister of our emperor."

"Lord Sonne, I fear there has been some mistake here. Did Shen, House Lord Frya, give you the impression that I agreed to any of your proposals?"

The ambassador waved his hand, "No, no. I have been in contact with others in your council. The majority of them signed the agreement."

"Really, who are these Lords, that hold my welfare so dear to their hearts?"

"Let me see. Ahh, yes, here is the agreement, all signed and legal." Lord Sonne handed Mar'ya a handful of papers.

She glanced down at the signatures, stood up, and headed for the council chambers.

"Come, Lord Sonne, you can personally witness my thanks to these House Lords."

Lord Sonne followed Mar'ya, a large, satisfied smile on his face.

Mar'ya, followed by her guards, entered the council chambers, glanced at the assembled

Lords and pointed to House Lord Leon, "Remove his head."

Her voice was calm. The guards looked at her, startled. When she nodded, one stepped forward and very expertly removed the head of Leon, House Lord Wav.

Mar'ya frowned, "Lord Leon always created such a mess wherever he went. He never learned that it is extremely bad manners to bleed all over the council chambers. Oh no, he got blood on my cake," She sighed loudly, "Throw it in the garbage, have cook bake another cake. Oh, and get the house cleaners in here."

She turned to face the other horrified House Lords, "Well then, who is next?" She asked mildly.

No one answered and she smiled, "Shall we discuss what you have all been up to in the last two months?"

After letting the silence draw out and watching her House Lords glance nervously at each other, Mar'ya raised her eyebrows and continued. "Gentlemen, I did ask you a question. Who gave you the authority to make concessions and agreements for Crystia? Last time I checked the law, that was the job of the Crystal Guardians and the Throne.

"So again, I ask: How dare you place your signature on this, this abomination?" She raised the papers in her hand over her head.

She turned to the soldiers who stood behind her, "Go to House Wav. Tell them what has happened and give them the option of following the path of their former Lord, or of swearing fealty to the Crystal Throne."

"If they refuse, Your Majesty?" One of the soldiers asked.

Mar'ya shrugged, "Take their boats, any food they have stored, and burn their homes to the ground." She turned back to the council, "Lord Leon was the best of you. He had courage. Leave my palace, return to your people and confess what you have done. Any of your House who wish to follow Crystal will be welcomed. The rest have three days to leave my kingdom. I do not care where you go or how you get there, but you will go, and you will go empty-handed. I have spoken. Hear me.

"Lord Sonne, may I suggest that you avail yourself of the services of those empire warships off-shore, and leave my kingdom?"

"You will regret this, young woman." Lord Sonne sputtered.

"Lord Sonne, you are not welcome in my nation, nor is your Lord Prevor and his multitude of wizards. I want all of you gone on the morning tide. Do you understand?"

"Insolent creature, to throw the goodwill of the empire in its face this way! You will rue the day you insulted the emperor."

"Lord Sonne, tell my half-brother this: If at any time the empire wishes to negotiate in good faith with the people of the eastern continent, we will listen to what he has to say. We will not, however, tolerate treachery, nor will we accept him encouraging our Lords to disobey the laws of our land.

"Please escort the ambassador to the harbor." Two of the soldiers snapped to attention and led the still sputtering High Lord Mervin Sonne of the Western Empire out of the city.

Mar'ya turned back to her stunned council, "Well?"

Twelve of the Lords glared at her as they filed angrily out of the room.

After a moment's silence, Mar'ya bowed her head. "Half of my Houses gone. Oh Crystal, defend us."

"It could have been worse, Your Majesty." Shen murmured.

"How? Tell me how?"

"You could have found out who the traitors were after they threw open the gates of the city. Most of the people love you. You do not stand alone."

"Shen, thank you for reminding me, I will grieve for the Houses that are lost to us, but I will strive twice as hard for the Houses that remain. I will not break faith with them. I am going to the chapel. Let me know when Alex arrives. Now, I need to be alone to think of what comes next."

As she stepped into the hall, she saw Barak striding toward the exit.

"Barak,"

"I am leaving."

Mar'ya shrugged, "Fare thee well, wizard."

"Cold, unnatural witch." He spat and stormed out of the castle.

*****

Shen, Alex and their guest moved through the silent castle. As they passed the chapel, heart-wrenching sobs from inside stopped them.

"How she suffers." The hooded, robed figure with Shen and Alex murmured.

Alex sighed, "Her burden none of us can take from her, Vera, no matter how we wish it otherwise."

"So wise, young Alex?" the robed one whispered.

"I had a good teacher." Alex's answer was short as he walked into the chapel.

"Weeping child of the weeping god. I'm sure there is a great ballad in there somewhere." Alex drawled.

"Pig." Mar'ya dug out a handkerchief and blew her nose. "When did you get back?"

"Attractive," Alex drawled, then continued in the same conversational tone, "A few hours ago. Wash your face and join us in your office."

An hour later, Mar'ya walked into her office. She gave a quick glance around the room, nodded at the robed figure in the corner, turned, and locked the door behind her.

"Wise child." Alex said, watching her closely.

"Of course. I am, after all, a Sultav." She said loftily. "Oh Alex. I am awful, I told the guard to chop off Leon's head and he did, just like that. Swish, head gone."

"Well, Leon needed his head cut off. Really, Mar'ya, he was a poisonous snake."

"I know, but I wish I could have done it myself instead of asking that poor young man to do it for me. He'll probably have nightmares from it."

Shen and Alex stared at her for a moment, then both started to laugh.

"It's not funny." She stamped her foot.

"Beloved queen, that young man was honored to serve you. He would have proudly beheaded every one of those Lords if you had asked it of him. He would die if you ask him."

"What am I doing to my people?" Mar'ya stared at Alex in horror.

"You are doing what your people demand of you: Supporting them, following the old ways, and most importantly, loving them. Each of them is a part of you, and you are a part of them. They love you. They would die for you, as you would die for them. It would, however, be much better if we all lived for each other."

Alex turned, and proudly said to the robed figure, "This is my queen. My Queen, may I present one who speaks for the nomads?"

Mar'ya flushed. The pride in Alex's voice touched her soul. "Welcome to the Crystal Palace." She said softly.

The robed one nodded, "You will do. There is steel in your body and great power in your mind. We will deal with you, Witch of the Crystal. Let there be honor between our people always."

"Then let us deal." Mar'ya sat behind her desk as the robed one spoke of what the desert people wanted in return for their help.

"So, I am to be sold on the auction block to the highest bidder. My people will lose their independence and my nation will be dissolved. The only difference is that our new overlords will at least live on the same side of the world as we. I cannot do this. I asked your help because when the empire has crushed us, you will be its next target. Can you not see that it is in your own best interest to help us?"

"We are the same people. Before the grieving, our people were one." The hooded face turned toward her.

"Shen?" Mar'ya glanced at her cousin.

"The nomad speaks the truth, but not all of it." There was deep anger in Shen's eyes.

"Man of the mountains, would you agree that each of us only knows one side of a story over a thousand years old? Would you also agree that constant contact with the wizards have weakened your tie to the grieving one?"

Shen closed his eyes, "Not in Frya. There, no wizard has ever walked, but in general, you may be right."

"Listen well, Crystal Witch, here is our deal: You will name our Ah'Jarl as your Champion, for this is not a war that can be won by force of arms alone. If either the desert or the city tries to defeat this enemy alone, we will both be crushed. All our people will perish, and our ways will be as dust."

Mar'ya winced. She walked to the window in her office and stared out over the city. At last, she returned to her desk. "For the life of my people, I will accept your Ah'Jarl as my Champion."

"Child, the city will remain as it has been. The old ways will stay, and the desert will remain as it has been. I swear to you, the old ways will stay." The nomad said solemnly.

"Can you swear this for your leader?"

"Can your Crystal Guardians swear for you?"

"Yes, for they speak with the voice of Crystal... Oh."

"Exactly."

Shen stood and opened the office door to the sound of bells as the twelve Crystal Guardians, also robed and hooded stepped in. The Crystal Guardians stared at the nomad three long minutes. Then they turned to Mar'ya, nodded, and left the room.

Mar'ya leaned forward, then instructed, "Shen, write: I, Mar'ya Olena Sultav, Holder of the Crystal Throne and queen of all Crystia, do swear to name the Ah'Jarl, greatest warrior mage of the Desert Nomads and leader of all the tribes, as my Champion. I give and bestow upon him all the rights, privileges, duties, and responsibilities that accompany the title of Champion. He will command the armies of Crystia, and do all in his power to ensure the health and well-being of the people. The old ways shall continue. Any daughter we should share will inherit the Crystal Throne. Our sons shall have free choice between the city and desert. Neither of us shall, in any way, coerce the people to change their ways or their beliefs. There will be honor between my people and his, and between his people and mine. This pact has been approved and witnessed by the Crystal Guardians."

Shen sighed, "I do not like this, but the Crystal Guardians have given me orders to sign in their names."

The Nomad nodded, "It is well written. Need you show it to your councilors?"

Mar'ya nodded, and Alex, his face solemn left the room.

He returned five minutes later with the other ten loyal House Lords, and locked the door as the last one entered.

Silently, Mar'ya handed the agreement to them. When they were through reading, they walked to the far side of the room, and spoke together in a whisper, then returned to the table.

"Well, Majesty, if that's what you want to do, none of us here has a problem with it, but I can tell you now, there will be those who will object." House Lord Evan spoke quietly.

Mar'ya glanced around the room, "Okay, Evan, who is going to object?"

"Oh, like I said not any of us in here, but when you threw out the Old House Lords, a group of the younger bucks stayed. After all, there was a single queen who would have to take a mate, and each of them thought they had as good a chance as the other."

Mar'ya blinked as she unraveled Evan's convoluted statement, then laughed shortly, "I'd sooner wed a snake." she spat. Then realized what she had said.

"Oh Crystal. That's torn it."

Laughter erupted in the room. Even the nomad representative chuckled.

"Under the circumstances, we will forgive you." The nomad said when the laughter died down.

"House Lords Frya, Tau, Orin, Sa, Capra, Sua, Agon, Trata, Sultav, Paron, Mar, and Kel are you willing to approve this contract between the people of the city and those of the desert?" Mar'ya watched the House Lords closely as she spoke. There was no hesitation in any of them as they leaned forward to affix their signatures to the papers.

"Well, that's that. We have about six months to finish making preparations. Good luck, people." Mar'ya started to stand when the nomad spoke again.

"One moment, where do you wish my people to stay?"

Mar'ya stared around the room, "Well the tribal leaders can stay here in the castle. We have enough room, but I..." She shook her head, "How much room is left in the western district?"

"Well we could hold about another two hundred, it'll be close quarters but the nomads are lot like us. They don't mind snuggling up to their neighbors." Pat grinned happily, while Mar'ya prayed that she misunderstood Pat's meaning.

"Umm, okay, where else?"

Alex grinned, "Don't worry, Highness, Crystal City can hold all of the tribes, and a little snuggling with your neighbor can be a good thing, especially on a cold winter's night."

"Alex!" Mar'ya blushed.

"Oh, I don't know, that sounds like a remarkably sane suggestion under the circumstances." The nomad interrupted, laughing.

"Fine, you work out living arrangements, I am going to get some rest." Mar'ya flounced out of the room.

I am so tired, so frightened. I hope this is the right thing for my people. It feels right; I can feel Crystal in my heart. She is not weeping anymore; she is alert and waiting for something; something that I need to do; oh Crystal, tell me what you want.

Chapter Eight

"You want me to do what?"

"Ah'Jarl, stop pacing, and pay attention!"

"Have you all gone mad? The four of you tell me that you have contracted our people to fight a war that is none of our concern, while I play perfumed stud to some spoiled city woman and I'm supposed to calm down?"

"'Quarl! I am Asan, elder of all the tribes of the desert. Next to me is Vera, Speaker of Stone, she who teaches the great magic to both warriors and mages, and your mother. Do you think either of us would take any action that would destroy our people?"

Vera sighed as she studied her son. In every way he was the opposite of the calm, young woman she had met in Crystia. "Sit down and listen. You claim this war is none of our concern; the people of Storm return to the east. They will finish the job their god started and destroy all of us. Crystia and Stoneland Desert would be no more. Is this truly what you wish to see happen?"

'Quarl dropped to one of the many cushions on the floor of the tent, ran his hand through long, golden hair and scowled.

"All right, so we help her fight the westerners. Afterward, we come home, back to the desert, the end."

Vera shook her head, "We do not have the strength to defeat Storm's people. If we cannot get the help of Crystal and Stone, we are doomed."

"Well, then we are doomed. Stone is sealed because of Crystal's betrayal, and Crystal spends all her time up in the mountains hiding behind Mist and weeping in remorse. Now you tell me to trust the word of her Witch Queen? No!"

"'When Stoneland and Crystia are one, then shall the seal be broken, and Stone shall be free once more.'" Vera quoted the old prophecy.

'Quarl sighed, "What is she like?"

"You have already met her. Don't you remember? Small, dark, arrogant, she loves her people more than herself. She is willing to do whatever it takes to protect all the people of the east, not just those of the Crystia, but those of the desert as well."

"She has fooled you, old woman." 'Quarl frowned, as a happy giggle echoed in his mind. He shook his head, dislodging the recurring memory, and turned his attention to what his mother was saying.

"Asan leaves to join her council in the morning. Already, six of the ten tribes have taken their warriors and their elders to the city."

"You did this without my permission?"

"This is the will of Stone. We do not need your permission. It does not matter what you feel or think. Stone's will must be followed. How do you think the witch feels? When those who speak with Crystal's voice came to her and said, 'You must do this,' she bowed her head and accepted. Is she wiser than you are? She sees the danger we face, and is willing to do whatever she must to protect a land she loves. Is she stronger willed than you are? She will even accept a dirty, scarred, stinking, desert nomad as her Champion to serve the lives and the faith of her people. Is she a better ruler than you are?

'Quarl scowled, "She realizes her people are weak, I don't blame her for trying to ally her people with ours. We do not need the city people. The desert warriors are strong; we can protect ourselves. You would have me chained to a woman who thinks of our people as stinking savages?"

Vera shook her head. "Did you not hear me? You have no choice. This is Stone's will." She wrinkled her nose, "I am sorry, My Son, but not only are you a stubborn idiot, but you stink of sweat and riding beast. Your hair is unkempt, and your beard looks like a goat's." Vera frowned, "I know our men pride themselves on their facial hair, but yours is a disgrace. Shave it off."

'Quarl stared at his mother in shock, "Mother! You shame me."

"Son, I love you. You are the protector of our people, our greatest warrior mage, but you are not perfect, and the will of Stone is greater than you are."

"I will think on this."

"Don't think too long, the Witch Queen estimated we have about six months to prepare, and one of those months has already passed."

"I will join the warriors in the city." 'Quarl stood and walked from the tent.

"You were a bit hard on him, Vera," Asan said mildly.

Vera shrugged, "He is my son, and all that I said was truth."

Asan bowed his head, "It was truth."

*****

'Quarl walked toward his tent, a frown on his face. He was so deep in thought he did not notice the large, red-headed warrior stalking him until it was too late to protect himself.

"Karl, damn you, give me some warning next time!" 'Quarl, mightiest warrior of the nomads, lay on his back gasping for breath.

"How much warning do you think the westerners will give you, oh great and mighty leader?" Karl shook his head, "Your reactions are slowing. Two years ago, no man in the desert could catch you unaware."

"You are not just anyone. Next to me, you are the best of our warriors. No westerner can match our skills." 'Quarl stood up next to his friend.

"Keep believing that and the nomads will be looking for a new Ah'Jarl." Karl shook his head and started to walk away.

"Karl, does my beard make me look like a goat?" 'Quarl called after his friend.

"No, not at all." Karl kept on moving away, "I could not honestly insult a goat by comparing it to you, though you do smell like one." Laughing, Karl disappeared behind a row of tents.

With a long-suffering sigh, the Ah'Jarl went to his tent to bathe and shave. It was going to be a bad year. *I am a warrior, not some perfumed courtier. I am supposed to smell like sweat and riding beast. It is not my fault that my beard doesn't grow.* He frowned at a young voice in his memory, *"I'm a boy, I'm supposed to smell bad."* Then shook his head, *I need to do some serious training or, when I reach the city, I will embarrass my people.*

For the next six weeks, 'Quarl traveled through the desert; training both his mind and body, studying the writings of his people, and honing his skills in both combat and tactics. He really did not believe the westerners would be that much of a problem. The desert warriors would defeat these soft city invaders easily. He grinned. *My mother is overreacting. She has listened to the cry of Crystia, and has forgotten the powers of her own people.*

On his way to the city, 'Quarl passed through the empty lands that ten weeks ago had been home to the Crystal Houses Tau and Orin. He frowned. *This witch really is frightened if she has brought even the most remote of her people into the city. Bah, now I have to go and pacify a terrified, hysterical female and find a way to control an overcrowded city whose populace has no love for my people.*

'Quarl kicked absently at a pebble in his path, as he surveyed the abandoned farmland before him. Even the animals were gone. "I wonder where they took the herds?" he muttered. "Probably to Frya lands."

A small sound caught his attention. He spun to see what it was and darkness enclosed him.

*****

When 'Quarl regained consciousness, he cautiously glanced around through barely opened eyes. He was in a large, white tent. The cot he lay on was its only furnishing. 'Quarl could sense no other human in the room with him, but that did not mean he was not under observation. His nostrils flared as he tested the air. He could discern the smell of the sea, riding beasts and the faint, lingering scent of magic.

He checked his memory hoping to find some clue as to where he was. To his surprise, there was no memory before his awakening. Tendrils of fear and anger started to wind themselves in his mind. Ruthlessly, he forced them down. This was not the time or the place for emotional response. He took control of his bodily functions, slowing his respiration and his heartbeat until any casual observer would have thought him dead.

Deep in his being, he felt a brief flare of wonder at the power he could exert over his body, then dismissed it. He began searching for any damage to his body. Everything was intact and in working condition. He moved his attention to his brain, still searching for physical harm. Again, he found no damage. He relaxed, and searched for damage to his psychic self. He went inward to the heart of all his memories, down the tracts that life had formed in his mind. He found the knowledge of how to do what he was doing, but no memory of how or where he learned the skill.

There was the knowledge of many methods of killing, both in defense and offense, but again, no memory of the learning of these skills. He found no memory of who or what he was, only the knowledge that he was a dangerous man with very few friends.

Deeper he went, following his mental paths further and further into his psyche until, at last, success. There were breaks that were not natural, but a forced burning out of the tracts in his brain; a thing that could only be done by magic. He knew instinctively that the memories he searched for had retreated far beyond the break.

In defense, his knowledge of who and what he was had tucked itself deep in the darkness at the heart of all life. To destroy that part of his memory, his body would have to die. He sighed. Now he must find a way to repair the damage or his full memories would never return.

Slowly, he reviewed the knowledge available to him until he found what he was looking for. A quiet sense of relief flooded him. He did have the skill needed to heal the damage done to him. If he moved this line here, and borrowed matter from there, it should work. He had done this before for others, but never for himself. At last, it was done. Now, all he needed was time for the new growth to take place. He hoped that time would be granted to him.

The man began a controlled awakening, carefully he sped up his heart and respiration, then extended his awareness outside his body. If not for his superb control, he would have betrayed himself, for there were others in the room with him. He extended his awareness even further outward...

"We should have killed him, Jarash. It's stupid keeping him alive. He'll never support the young Emperor. Why should he when the Witch has named him Champion? What can we offer this stinking desert rat to equal that?"

"Rede, be quiet. We need offer him nothing. Our Emperor doesn't need a mindless drone, and that's all he is now. The queen's forces will dwindle to naught when they see what our master has done to the most powerful of her allies." Quiet laughter greeted that comment.

"Maybe we should send the mindless rat back to the lady?" someone else suggested.

"Don't be a fool, we'll take no chances." This was a new voice.

Again the laughter. "We could send him back, Your Highness." The man on the couch shivered, this new voice was as cold as the winter winds in the northern desert. "If you wish to humiliate your sister, Lord Gregor, we could chain her Champion and send him to her a drooling, mindless idiot. In twenty-four hours, not even the gods will be able to help him. As for your sister, she is not as great a witch as she thinks. We have seen to that."

"Twenty-four hours? Can you guarantee that he will stay this way, Wizard Bunji?"

"Yes, Lord Gregor. No power that we know of will be able to cure him after one day."

"Then do as you will."

There was a breath of sea air as the tent flaps opened. He lay still. He could still sense others in the tent with him.

"If he doesn't awaken in twenty-four hours, we'll know that the treatment has been successful, then we can return the lady's ugly pet to her. Our people in the palace can keep an eye on him, not that it should be necessary." The wizard instructed, then laughed cruelly as he too, left the room.

A few moments later, the sound of feet moving away from him, soft laughter, and the slight disturbance of the air currents, told 'Quarl that the last of his jailers had left the tent. *I woke up just in time. An hour later and it truly would have been too late for me to repair the damage inside my mind. I must keep any sign of repair hidden. Any examination must still show the break. So, I am someone's champion, someone who is depending on me for help.* A bitter laugh slid through his mind and anger danced along his nerve endings. Once more, he wrestled with his emotions. *I wish I could remember more, but I dare not disturb the still healing tracts in my mind. For now, I will work on hiding the rebuilding and the new growth going on. I know who my enemies are. First, I must heal myself, then I will attend to this Lord Gregor and his wizards.*

Chapter Nine

In the heart of Crystal City stood the Crystal Palace, its four towers reaching high into the heavens. The Witch Queen, Mar'ya Olena Sultav, holder of the Crystal Throne, watched the river that flowed through the city with a frown on her face, and ignored the playful breeze that stirred her long, brightly-colored gown. A small sound disturbed her concentration and she turned to her companion.

"Shen, how is the city?"

"Crowded."

"Shen, I know that you are setting all sorts of records being the first male Crystal Guardian, and the first male House Frya Lord, but could you not start making cryptic comments just yet? Now, how is the city."

"The city is crowded. If you mean how are the people, then ask that."

Mar'ya sighed, "Shen, how are my people faring?"

Shen was silent for a moment, "Did you know that Barak was still in the city?"

"What is he doing?"

"Causing mayhem. He has managed to encourage some of the young nobles to join him in harassing the nomads, in spreading rumors and stirring fear in the people. They are telling the people that you choose a desert rat instead of a western lord, and the war is all your fault. If we force the nomads out of the city, well, the empire will bring you a more suitable mate, and then they will go home,"

"Kill him."

"Highness, that may not be wise."

Mar'ya stared over her city, then nodded. "Ring the bells."

Shen gave her a startled look. "Highness, are you sure?"

"Yes. I have made an error, I spoke to the House Lords, but I did not speak to the heart of my people. Sound the bells. Tomorrow, I will speak to my people. Afterward, find that wizard and kill him. Oh, and get me a list of those brainless young nobles following him."

Shen moved to stand beside Mar'ya, "Years ago, these westerners would not have dared attack us. Our witches would have quickly sent them back to their own land. Now there are so few of us. I fear for our people, cousin."

Mar'ya nodded, "Only fourteen of us are left. The twelve named Crystal Guardians, Pat House Lord Orin, and me. Shen, why is the birth-rate for witches so low?"

"Your Highness, needs only look to the wizards for your answers."

Mar'ya glanced at her cousin and chief-advisor, then stared out over the river again. The silence on the tower was broken only by the sound of the river rushing down to the sea.

She sighed, "It is past time. My Champion must be dead. If he lived, he would be here by now. But how and who? Surely not my worthless brother? None of his serpents could possibly defeat my Champion."

"Ambush, maybe, My Lady," the other suggested.

The woman shrugged. "I hope not. That would imply carelessness on my Champion's part and would not bode well for our future."

"As you say, Mar'ya," Shen said sharply.

She turned her eyes from the river and looked down where the harbor section of her city gleamed white in the moonlight. The makers of the Crystal City had used highly polished, white, triangular blocks to create the buildings. In the center of the city, stood the tall, thin, pure crystal spires of the palace. The spires reflected all light, and from a distance, it seemed as if the whole city was surrounded by rainbows.

Mar'ya's eyes burned, "How I love my city." She whispered. "Those siege weapons of my brother will shatter and destroy centuries of labor. If I cannot stop him, all this beauty will be gone. Shen, you know that I'm oath-bound not to use magic in this war with my brother. I need this Ah'Jarl, Warrior Mage of the Desert, for he can do what I cannot, by law, do. He can search out and destroy any spies that still remain in my court."

"Lady, I can see no future good coming of this alliance. What if this Ah'Jarl has been killed on the way here? How do you think his people would react?"

"Alive or dead, he still serves my purpose. If my brother kills him, then the desert people will be our allies in vengeance. I will be able to stand before the Crystal Guardians and demand they let me use magic, for how else would the greatest mage in the land be killed, save by magic? If he's alive, then I won't need my powers, I'll just use his."

Mar'ya shivered, "Come Shen, let us go inside where it is warm. I don't think my Champion will be arriving tonight."

With a last wistful glance around her, Mar'ya led her cousin down from the tower.

Early the next morning, the bells in Crystal City rang, calling the people together in the large plaza before the castle.

"I don't know if you've noticed, but there is an army outside of our walls." Mar'ya began, and paused while nervous laughter rippled briefly through the crowd.

"I'm sorry I did not talk to you. I left it to your House Lords. I forgot that you needed me to tell you what I was doing. So here is what is going on: The empire wishes to swallow us, you all know this. They have no interest in who we are or what we believe. They would force us all to believe as they do. They would insist that we turn away from Crystal, abandon the old ways; no longer honor the Crystal Guardians. Our women would lose their freedom and we would no longer exist as the people of Crystal. I called on the nomads of Stoneland to help us fight this threat. The people of the desert share this land with us, and the invasion of the empire threatens them also.

"The beliefs of the nomads and ours are both based on the old ways. We are cousins; any who would disparage them, would also disparage us. All of you, at one time or another, have heard the western lords refer to us as barbarians. Now is not the time for we of the east to be fighting amongst ourselves. When we defeat the empire and this war is over, you and they can go into the wild and bash each other with your fists until you all fall down with exhaustion."

A woman, in the crowd, yelled, "So, you marrying their leader?"

Mar'ya grinned, "Have you seen their men?"

"I'll take him if you change your mind." The woman yelled and the crowd laughed; genuine laughter this time.

"That was well handled." Shen complimented her as they walked to her office.

"Have you found the wizard?" Mar'ya frowned.

"Not yet." Shen stopped, "Mar'ya what is bothering you?"

"Oh, let me see, there is an army outside my walls, traitors inside my walls, my Champion is missing, and Crystal is sending me cryptic dreams. Did I miss anything?" She growled.

"Ahh, the joys of being queen. By the way, Alex is back and he wants to meet with you in your quarters later tonight." Shen smiled sympathetically.

Mar'ya nodded. "Probably more bad news," she grumbled.

When she reached her rooms later that night, she found Alex stretched out on her bed fast asleep. "Why am I always finding my cousins in my bed?" Mar'ya asked as she threw a pillow at him.

Alex opened one eye and sat up slowly, "Maybe because you work us so hard we have forgotten where our own beds are."

Mar'ya sat next to Alex, "I'm sorry. There is no one else I trust."

"Wait until you get my bill." Alex groaned, "I have not slept in two weeks."

"So, what have you found out?"

"Well, the Ah'Jarl disappeared in Orin territory."

"Do you think some one from House Orin arranged that?"

"No. The easiest way to reach the city from the desert is through Orin lands."

"So, Barak and his sycophants probably notified the Western Lords that he was on his way. After that, all they had to do was wait for him to show up." Mar'ya sighed and flopped down on her bed next to Alex.

"Barak is still in the city?" Alex was suddenly very alert.

"Yes, Shen found out yesterday. He is running around causing trouble."

"So what are you doing?"

"I want him dead. I want the names of those young idiots who are following him. I want a good night's sleep; I want peace and harmony, and I want my Champion to appear." Mar'ya closed her eyes, "Go away; I want to sleep forever."

Alex smiled, and pulled the covers up around her.

"Sleep, beloved cousin," he whispered before closing the door behind him.

*****

Two days later, Mar'ya was called to the walls of Crystal City to speak with the emissaries of the western army.

"Queen, behold your Champion, Desert Warrior, and greatest warlock in your land." They shoved a slack-jawed, shuffling giant with a chain around his mighty neck to the ground before the gates, as they rode off laughing.

"Bring me one the Desert Elders." Mar'ya commanded, and one of her guards ran off to obey.

"Is that your Ah'Jarl?

When the elder fell on his knees and wept, she accepted that this shell was indeed her Champion. Since he still lived, she was stuck with him, but she would make her brother pay dearly for this.

With a curt nod, she walked away, calling over her shoulder, "Open the gates and give the man to the care of his people."

The queen watched the desert chiefs, who were a part of her court tend gently to the man they called Ah'Jarl, Master of The Desert. The men's faces were taut with anger and grief. They spoke softly to each other in their own language, ignoring her. She was not used to being ignored, but then, these desert men were not her vassals. They were her allies, and the tie that bound them together was her promise to name their Ah'Jarl as her Champion and future mate.

She agreed because she saw no other way to win her throne. Thanks to her brother, she had the means to win her throne by magic, but was stuck with a mindless shell for a mate. The Crystal Guardians would have to give her permission to use magic now.

The door of the inner sanctum was opened by a young woman in the white and silver robes of a named Guardian. "May I help you?" She asked softly.

"I wish to speak with the Guardians."

The young woman bowed, "I will let them know you are here, Majesty."

Mar'ya gave little attention to courtesy once she was in the presence of the Crystal Guardians. "Crystal Guardians, my brother has used magic to reduce my Champion to an idiot. I should no longer be restrained."

"Daughter of Crystal, have you not yet learned patience?" The eldest of the Unnamed Guardians asked softly.

Mar'ya sighed, "Tell Crystal to learn patience. She sends me dreams all night, and wails in my head while I'm awake. I'm tired of it. I thought you people were supposed to be the ones talking to her, not me. Now, my Champion has been delivered at the city gates with his mind completely gone. His people walk the hallways of the castle and the streets of the city, wailing death chants. I beg the Guardians pardon if they think I have been hasty in my reaction."

"Child, your sarcasm will not work with us. We understand your reasons, however, and forgive your rudeness. The restriction on your use of magic is no longer in force. May Crystal grant you the power to achieve your goal."

Mar'ya bowed, and stamped out of the room her temper not at all soothed by getting her way. *The restriction on my using magic has been removed. Wonderful, except for the fact that I have no magic. Everyone calls me the Crystal Witch, but I am no witch. Barak called me barely competent, and he was right. Even after all his training, I know less than I did at sixteen. Now, I have to do this alone. I must protect both the people of Crystal and the people of Stone. I am afraid, but I must try. I cannot fail the people. Unlike Crystal, I will not abandon them to go wailing into the mountain. I will do what I can. I must tell my allies that I am not able to help them.* Mar'ya stopped walking as that thought came into her mind. *No, no, I will do it. I will ask them what to do, then I will do it.*

The hard-faced men with their wild hair and massive bodies bristling with strange weapons were so different from the slender, clean-shaven men of her people, that Mar'ya felt a small shiver of fear as she approached them. She straightened her back and stuck her chin out. No wonder her people called the desert nomads savages, she thought, glancing at their plain, brown pants and tunics.

As she approached the group around the Ah'Jarl's bed, Asan stepped forward to meet her. "One of your people is responsible for the betrayal of our Lord. This is truth. You will find the traitors and give them to us. For as the Ah'Jarl is ours, so are those who would rob him of that which is dearer than life."

Mar'ya tightened her lips. She was not used to being addressed in such a manner. She glared at the old man, then looked at the man lying on the bed. She could not hold them full blame. They had right on their side and her father had taught that one must deal fairly with allies, holding back anger until they were no longer allies.

"I hear thee. I'll do my best to find the ones you desire. You'll have them after I'm finished with them," she ended savagely.

The men looked at each other in silence then nodded at her. 'Ulan of the Northern Tribes gave her a grim smile, "Lady, please leave enough of the unfortunate ones for our pleasure," he said, startling her into a laugh.

Mar'ya took a deep breath, and spoke quickly before she lost her courage, "I would ask your elders to join my council. We must plan our next move." She glanced at the Ah' Jarl, "He can no longer act as Champion, I'll accept a substitute. Give me another of yours to act in his stead." She said, her eyes on a slender, young northern tribesman. The young man blushed and the others laughed.

"Nay, Lady, the Ah'Jarl is the only one among us who may do this. The Champion has accepted. As he has said, so be it. None may say no to his laws." Asan, the eldest of the tribesmen chided.

"Why did he accept?" she asked. The queen knew why she accepted, but she was curious as to why the mage warrior agreed.

"Lady, we have long had a prophecy that foretold the end of the wars between your people and ours. 'The time for peace will come with the mating of the mage and the witch. Their children will lead the world in peace for as long as they worship the light.' So spoke our Stones. When your offer came, our Speakers said, 'So shall it be,' and the mage warrior agreed."

"What are these stones you speak of?" Mar'ya had heard of the talking stones of the desert before, but ignored the story. She wondered if she might have made a mistake in dismissing them as superstitious rumor.

"A small thing of the desert. The Ah'Jarl will bring you to them at the proper time."

"The Ah'Jarl can't bring himself across the room. How do you expect him to do anything for me? Look at him. By Crystal, the man has no mind left. You are going to have to find yourself another Ah'Jarl. This one is useless to both of us. I most certainly won't accept him as Chosen."

"As you have said, so shall it be. We do not release you from the word that was given. He is still the Ah'Jarl," Asan glared at her.

The young queen wrinkled her nose in disgust and spun away, "I shall go and find your traitors," she snapped. As she walked away, a small, blond boy in her memory crossed his eyes and stuck his tongue out at her.

Chapter Ten

"Shen, where are you? Damn your hide, Shen!"

"Here Lady." The courtier looked at his queen with a frown.

"The desert chiefs claim that there are traitors in our midst who have caused their Ah' Jarl's present predicament. They want the traitors, and I have agreed that whatever is left of them when I am through, belongs to the desert nomads. Now get me a list of those young noblemen whom you claim have gone to my brother's camp. Oh, and I would give our allies Barak's bloody head."

Shen winced. "I hear thee, Lady." He bowed and rushed off to do his lady's bidding.

His discreet knock on the queen's chamber door stopped her pacing.

"That was quick. Do you have list already?"

"Lady can you trust young Anar, House Sul? Remember how loudly he cried when you named your Champion? I just wondered if any list he created would be worth the paper it was written on."

"I hear thee, Shen. What a mess these desert rats have gotten me into."

"Mar'ya don't you start saying things like that, not even behind your own doors. Also, remember that you invited them here."

Mar'ya nodded shortly. "Is there anyone left in the palace that I can trust besides you, Alex and the desert tribesmen? Ahh, Shen, the empire may name them rats, but their loyalty to their Ah'Jarl is a great virtue, and it is one I envy. I wish my more civilized Lords were as loyal to me."

"Highness, do not forget the Houses that serve you. Do not condemn us all because of the actions of young Lords who belong to Houses already proven traitorous."

Mar'ya sighed, "You are right, Shen. My loyal Houses, the ones I'm fighting for, do not deserve to be insulted because others misbehave."

She rubbed her head, "I am so very tired. Shen, go to the desert elders, and request guards from among their people to work with Mar and Kel warriors. Then bring me 'Ulan of the North. I would have him work closely with us."

When he arrived at her rooms, 'Ulan, was accompanied by six tribesmen and one of the elders. Mar'ya frowned, then rubbed her head. "Forgive me, I do not mean to be abrupt, but, 'Ulan, I thought I requested your attendance in my chambers?"

'Ulan answered, "Lady, as you requested, I'm here. The elder and these guards are my witnesses to the people of the Ah'Jarl that no matter what future claims are made, I have not betrayed my Lord. What do you wish?" 'Ulan bowed.

Mar'ya frowned briefly in displeasure. She refused to be stuck with that disgusting hulk they named Ah'Jarl for the rest of her days. The slender, elegant 'Ulan was much more pleasing to her eyes. If she must have a desert mate then this one would do much better than the large, scarred man in the other room.

"I want 'Ulan to work with my cousin, Alex Sultav. Also, I would turn over the security of my palace to the Northern Desert tribe working with Houses Mar and Kel." She sighed, "Alex does not keep normal hours, and many of our meetings are held in my personal quarters. These meetings are private, you will not be allowed to bring a bodyguard with you." She knew that she was not presenting her case tactfully, but she was tired. "If you accept the position, do not betray my trust. When you have sniffed out the traitors in our midst, I want to be the first to know, then you may report to your people."

The young man was quiet, then he turned to the Elder, "How say you, Elder? Is this oath fitting?"

The Elder studied Mar'ya for a moment, then nodded. "We know Alex, and respect him." The old man paused, "It is fitting, 'Ulan, if you swear only this to the queen. It is well that one of ours was chosen, and 'Ulan is known for his stealth and cunning." The Elder turned to the

Mar'ya and bowed, "We hear thee, Lady, and obey." He accepted formally.

Mar'ya was not happy that the old man gave the pledge. Now, she had no hold on 'Ulan. The elder would be responsible to their people for this oath and she would not be able to use it as wedge between 'Ulan and the other tribesmen. She also didn't like the comment about 'Ulan's personality. Could she have been so wrong in her judgment? The thought that she might have made an error shook her more than she cared to admit. For security reasons, it was good, but it could spell the end of her personal plans.

"As I have said, so be it. The announcement will be made at supper. Be prepared for trouble then." Mar'ya turned away, missing the smiles that flashed between the men in the room.

During supper, Mar'ya sat at the head of her table and watched the antics of her noblemen. *They remind me of a flock of brightly-colored birds, just as flighty, and just as useless,* she thought bitterly. On the other side of the table sat the Crystal Guardians. *They will be of no help to me in the coming conflict, for they are sworn to remain neutral. Their only duty is to set the rules and make sure that those rules are adhered to. After the conflict, they will verify the winner. No, the trouble will come from my young noblemen.*

They will object to my replacing one of them with a desert rat. How many more of them will forsake me and go to my brother, taking their personal armies with them? I cannot afford to lose too many. Even though I can easily win with the aid of the desert tribes, I can lose the support of my own people. I need that support if I am to rule effectively.

Damn my half-brother anyway. The Crystal Throne is mine by right, as it was my mother's before me. How dare this son of my father's first wife try to take my birthright away from me? Why was he not satisfied with his kingdoms across the sea? What does he need my small country for? Still, if I do not have the strength to keep what is mine the Crystal Guardians will give it to my brother.

I am going to have to prove again my fitness to rule. At twelve, I had my first testing, searching for the power that proclaimed me a witch and true claimant to the Crystal Throne. I passed that one easily. Now, twelve years later, I am again being tested. My powers are not yet fully matured, and according to my tutor, they will not be until I am thirty. There were so many forces that Barak has advised me not to try to control because of my youth. Now, I don't know if I can trust Barak's words. Would he have lied to me about my training? Oh Crystal, guide me. I am so confused. She sighed, w*ell I have no choice. I will do what I must, and damn the consequences.* She braced herself, rang the small bell by her plate for silence, and stood.

"There are traitors among us," she began. "Those traitors are responsible for the harm done our Champion. The desert warriors, as is their right, have demanded the heads of these traitors. These traitors are noblemen, and our chief of security is a nobleman. It is not fitting that a man should have to betray his friends and peers. Therefore, until this issue has been cleared, 'Ulan of the Northern Tribes, along with warriors of Mar and Kel will act as security. The quicker we find these traitors, the sooner everything can return to normal."

She sat down and waited for the objections to begin. Before the storm broke, however, the door to the dining hall was opened by a young warrior wearing House Kel colors. He walked over to the Nomad Elder Asan, "By command of my queen, I have a gift, my Lord Asan, to our allies of the desert from the warriors of Crystal." He bowed and placed a large box in front of Asan.

Asan opened the box, looked inside and smiled. "Young warrior of the city, the desert accepts your gift. Please give your queen and your brothers our thanks." He then closed the box and handed it to one of Nomads nearby. "Take this out and share it with the tribes." He instructed.

One of the young noblemen immediately objected, "If our queen is trying to bribe you people into staying in the city, we have a right to know what part of the treasury she is giving away." He smirked, "So, why don't you share this gift with all of us."

Mar'ya glanced at the Kel warrior. He grinned and winked at her. *What are my warriors up to now? I know they get along well with the nomads. Crystal, most of Kel warriors have nomad blood, but I wish they would warn me when they are going to play a prank.*

A gasp ran around the table as Asan reached into the box and calmly placed Barak's head on the table. Four of the young nobles ran out of the room, losing their supper on the way, while the other six sat frozen, pale, and shaken. Mar'ya laughed. It was a nervous reaction, and totally inappropriate. She covered her mouth with her hands, while her eyes assessed the reactions of her younger House nobles.

"Your Highness, I am Anar, House Sul, your palace security and I find this incident and most especially, your reaction to it, barbaric. Barak was a good, honest man. He was your tutor, and spent many years searching for wo-men with power to be trained. He did nothing to deserve this treatment."

"You are Anar. There is no longer a House Sul. Barak was a member of the empire. He was a wizard, and, using his power, he obtained information and passed it on to our enemies." Mar'ya stopped. Her eyes narrowed as she remembered Shen's earlier warning. Barak had led the search for witches in Crystia. Now there were none. "Barak and his wizards have been sealing the minds of our women for years. How many times have we heard them say that women should not hold power? They believed that only men were worthy. Now you, Anar, stand before me and name him an honorable man? Explain yourself."

"I need give no explanation to one who would refuse an honorable marriage with a lord of high standing in the empire, and ally herself with these filthy rats."

Silence descended on the room and Mar'ya sighed, "Anar, you make the late Leon of House Wav seem a total genius. I am sorry. However, I will give you a choice: Go out of my city, join those westerners you love so much, and let Crystal mourn the loss of your House; or place your head on the table next to the man you so admired."

Pat, Lord of Farming House Orin, stood and stared at the six young lords still in the room. "I've seen you, all of you, running around the western district making fun of the smaller Houses, calling us rat bait and squatters, but we ignored you. We thought you were just angry about the loss of status you suffered because of the actions of your elders. None of us thought you would sink so low as to betray Crystal, or her people. You don't deserve to live. None of you. But our queen, well, she is a gentle woman, who has given you the chance to leave the city alive. Take her offer. For if any of us see you walking the streets of the city, we will kill you." Pat cleared her throat, "Sorry, Highness, I hope my blunt language didn't upset you none."

Mar'ya gave Pat a sweet, gentle, loving, and entirely fake smile. "You are forgiven." She murmured, and watched in amusement as the young nobles quickly left the palace.

The amusement, however, quickly faded as she looked around the room, "We are all that is left: The seven smallest of the Crystal Houses; House Frya which has less than three hundred members; and the merchants."

Evan laughed, "Don't need no more. We have good allies, sharp minds, and a queen we love. It's enough."

'Ulan stood, "My people, the Northern Desert tribe, will work with your warriors to provide security for the palace and the city. In this, we'll serve the queen well." The young man grinned, exposing teeth filed to sharp points, and added, "There will be no more secrets leaked from this city."

As she left the room, she whispered to 'Ulan, "Meet me in your master's rooms with your elders in one hour. We must talk."

He nodded as she swept out, closely followed by Shen and six, large, well-armed tribesmen.

An hour later, she entered the Ah'Jarl's rooms. The Elders and Chiefs of the tribes were already waiting for her.

"We are probably under the surveillance of my brother's magicians. Do you know someplace we may go so that our conversation can be private?"

The men looked at each other, then nodded. 'Ulan said, "Talk, Lady. None but us will hear what is said in this room. Think thee that we would keep our Lord in a room not secure?"

"I have chosen my new head of security wisely." She turned to the others in the room. "I have reason to believe Barak was betraying me longer than just the last three months. I also believe his betrayal reached further than just passing information." Mar'ya closed her eyes. When she continued, her pain was evident in her voice. "He was a wizard of much power, a member of the Wizard Council and my tutor in the magic arts. If the Wizard Council is against me, we'll have no chance of victory. I'm not yet matured in my powers. At least, this is what

Barak told me, but now I'm beginning to doubt his word. I think he was holding me back on orders of the Council. My training isn't yet complete, and I must have full command of all my powers if we're to win the upcoming battle."

She looked at the solemn faces around her, then started when Asan, the oldest of the desert elders came to her and placed his hands on her head.

"Relax, Witch, I'll not harm thee, but if your powers are similar to ours, we can arrange for you to be trained with our people. It will be a risk, and you must find a way to leave the palace, but maybe it will work."

Mar'ya stood still under the old man's probing touch and felt him delve deep in her mind. She felt his sudden flare of distrust as he discovered her thwarted plans to seduce 'Ulan, and his shiver of anger as he found her thoughts concerning the Ah'Jarl. He stepped away from her.

"Witch, what I have found in your heart is between us. I'll tell none unless you endanger the unity of my people. As for your powers, they're fully matured. You were right to distrust your tutor. Go to my people and they'll finish teaching you what you need to know. Many of the women from your country have lived, worked and studied among the desert tribes."

"Why would your people train me? There is little trust and even less love between us. What would you gain from this?"

"If you're untrained, then the Ah'Jarl will not have a mate worthy of him."

Mar'ya nodded, "How long will it take?"

Asan shook his head. "Why is youth so impatient? It will take as long as it takes. Some things cannot be hurried."

"Old man, my city is under attack, my nobles are betraying me, and you prattle of youth's impatience. I don't have a lot of time. The minute my half-brother finds out I am no longer in the palace, he will move against my people."

"This is true, Crystal Witch, so then you'll have to learn quickly, won't you? Go and work hard. You have a great strength and much power. Also, your early training was good. It won't take you as long as it has some of the others."

Mar'ya grimaced. How was she going to get away from the Crystal Palace and reach the safety of the desert without being caught by her brother? It wasn't going to be easy, but then nothing lately had been.

She nodded to the elders, "I'll work on it. While I'm gone, I'll leave you, Asan, to sit on the council in the palace. You're the only ones I think I can trust not to hand over my crown, scepter, and throne to my half-brother; or even worse, to start a war that we are not yet ready to fight. Do you think that you can handle that without alienating the remainder of my nobles?"

The desert men looked at each other in surprise and Asan bowed low, "May we suggest, Lady, that you leave Shen, House Frya, in control. Make it known that we of the desert would support him as we would you. Surely, that would be the wiser course? We aren't diplomats and you'd come back to find your palace in shambles were it left to us."

"You would work with Shen?"

"He is your brother." Asan stated.

"He is my cousin." Mar'ya corrected.

Asan shrugged, "As you wish. We trust him, and he's loyal to you, Lady."

"I hear thee." Her mind was already selecting and discarding plans to get out of the city.

She would have to talk with Shen. As she started to leave the room, she stopped and turned to ask, "How can you be so sure that this room is secure?"

"You will learn that when you reach our people, Lady. It's only a minor magic." The elder smiled at her.

Mar'ya walked slowly back to her rooms her forehead furrowed in thought. *My tutor taught me that, against the eavesdropping of the Wizard Council, there was no protection. He added that none was necessary because the wizards had better things to do with their time than spy on common people. Yet these desert folk just told me that their simple magic was capable of securing a room against the wizards. Something is wrong. Either my tutor knew nothing of the desert, or he lied to me about the power of the wizards.* Neither prospect was comforting.

When she reached her rooms, Shen was waiting for her.

"Crystal Guardian Shen, are you developing mage powers that you know when I need to see you even before I send for you?" She smiled.

"Mar'ya there are problems," Shen replied seriously. A frown crossed his handsome face as he ran his fingers through his already artfully-tousled, black hair.

She sighed, "Shen, there are always problems. I'm dealing with a group of men who think they would be more comfortable with a man ruler; with wizards that I suspect of treachery; with a group of desert tribesmen who do not quite trust my intentions toward them; what else could possibly go wrong?"

"Should the desert men trust you?"

She chewed her lower lip thoughtfully, then nodded, "Yes. As long as they keep faith, so will I. It's necessary."

Shen looked at her for a moment then bowed, "As my Lady says."

She laughed, "Are you doubting my honor, Shen?"

"No, cousin." He looked horrified that she would even think such a thing.

Mar'ya shook her head. Shen was a faithful courtier and a good friend, but he had very little humor. "What did you want to discuss with me?" She sat down and gestured for him to do the same.

"Mar'ya, you're right to distrust the wizards. I believe at least four members of the Wizard Council were responsible for what happened to the Mage Warrior. Why did you suspect them?"

She bent her head and took deep breaths. There was a dread deep inside her. No one was strong enough to fight the whole Wizard Council. She was going to lose her throne.

"Oh Shen, I thought maybe one or two of them, not the whole council. Barak for certain. Some of the things he taught me for years, I've just discovered to be false." She lifted her head and stared at Shen in horror, "Shen, my father chose this tutor for me after my mother died. He laid the groundwork for this. My father never intended for me to win this battle. He wanted it all for his son. Tell me true, is that why he married my mother?"

Shen stared at her for a moment, then sighed. "Richard, Lord of the West, came from a land where men ruled and had all the power.

The marriage between him and your mother was negotiated by the Wizard Council. Your mother wanted one of her own noblemen, but the trade agreements that your father brought were too lucrative to our country for Belia to refuse."

"Shen, can I trust you? You were my father's man."

"Never, Mar'ya. If your mother had done as she wished, my father and she would have been wed. Your father asked me to keep you safe, and that oath, I gladly swore. Always, Mar'ya, I have put what was best for you before any promises made, other than those I made to your mother and my father. 'A Crystal Witch must rule from the towers or the kingdom will fall.' This is the prophecy House Frya serves. These foreign men and the wizards deem their strength greater than those of the gods that ordained the fate of Crystia, and that is a dangerous mistake, cousin."

The queen closed her eyes. This wasn't the time for tears. Later, she would weep for the father she never really knew. She knew that he did not love her, but to learn that he had actively worked to destroy her and all she held dear, hurt. She finally had proof that he used her mother and betrayed his daughter, all because he wanted power for his son. One day, she would weep until the tears ran dry, but not now. There was no time now.

"Shen, I must get out of the palace for a while. So much has happened, I need to be alone and think of all I have learned this day. I must go to Frya and visit the temple that holds Crystal's presence. While I'm gone, you'll be in charge. The men of the desert will help you in any way necessary."

She was proud of herself. She had no doubt that her room was under surveillance and the whole conversation was overheard by some member of the wizard council. She had given the perfect excuse to leave the palace, everyone would think that she was going to grieve over her father's betrayal. *I can wait, and one day I will take revenge on all those who have betrayed me and mine.*

Shen bowed low at the waist, "Mar'ya I'm sorry to have added to your pain, but you had to know. I fear now is not a good time for you to be leaving Crystal City."

"I must go, Shen. There is too much for me to deal with. I must go to the Crystal Mountain. Will you help me?"

"I will try to do as you command cousin. How long will you be gone?"

"As long as it takes."

After Shen left her, Mar'ya stood before her window and looked down on her city. *Oh my people, hold on just a while longer. Continue to trust me. I have no doubts that Shen will do a good job while I am away. If Shen tries to betray me, I will return from the desert to find his head gracing the walls. Shen, you are my dearest cousin. My mother loved you like a son. If you betray me, I will never trust again. The men of the desert do not love me, but they are men of honor. That is all I want, for how can I trust those who claim to follow me for love when my own father found it so easy to betray me? No, I will trust in the honor of the desert and, when this mess is over, I will examine closely where my life will lead. I do know one thing: If the nomads keep faith, then so will I, even if it means marrying the drooling idiot who is now their Lord.*

The Council of Wizards is fighting on my brother's side. I am sure this plot is not a recent one. The wizards conceived it even before my mother's time. My father and half-brother are only pawns in their game. The wizards do not believe that my brother would be a better ruler than I. They are rebelling against the rule of women with powers equal to, or greater than, their own. She smiled bitterly, *no wonder they encouraged hostilities with the nomads, for desert magic is strong among both men and women, and all with the power are trained. I am not certain the Wizard Council knows this, but I am sure they suspect.*

With a small shrug, she shook off her thoughts. *There is no time now for wondering about the intentions of the wizards. When I return from the desert, I will deal with them. Now, I have to find a way to leave the palace and get to the desert so I can finish my training. I wonder if there is a law somewhere that states all my choices must be hard ones?*

*****

Four hours later, a group of desert women entered Mar'ya's quarters. They combed her long, black hair into the nomad women's trademark braids, and exchanged her bright, silk gown for their own tan pants and tunic. When they left an hour later, the group was larger by one, but no one paid any attention to the laughing desert women. Mar'ya was taken to the far eastern section of the palace grounds where some of the tribesmen made their camp.

Asan waited for her. "Lady, you have two hours of protection. After that time, we can no longer shield the fact that you're missing from the palace. You must make the most of your time and get as far away as possible. All'ya will travel with you and be your guide." Asan pointed to a tall, young woman wearing desert browns and the large curved sword of her people, "Queen, give us a name."

The queen thought a while. "I'll be traveling as one of your people, so I'll use a name similar to those your women have. Call me Mar'ya. It's a good name and one of my own." The queen smiled.

Asan nodded, "It is good. Where you go now you'll no longer be the crystal witch, but only Mar'ya of no rank or riches; just a lowly student touched by the power. Remember this, and act accordingly," he warned, and turned away from the group.

Chapter Eleven

'Quarl, the Ah'Jarl, lay placidly on his bed. He thought about what he heard earlier and marveled at the scope of the forces arrayed against the Witch Queen of the Crystal Towers. He touched the minds of his people and knew they doubted the Witch could be trusted completely. When she spoke as Crystal Witch, ruler of Crystia, or as Lady of the Tower, they had faith in her words. As a woman, they trusted her not at all. He scowled. Soon, he would have to deal with all three faces of her and he must learn more.

He was pleased that his people were here, for when they touched him, a small bridge was formed and their knowledge became his. These were not true memories, only borrowed ones, but they would do for now. The queen was an arrogant woman, and he sensed the impatient power that seethed within her. Her sense of humor was very strange. He smiled. She would make a fitting mate for him.

They would deal well together, not peacefully, but well. For now, there was nothing he could do but wait and hope that his arrogant lady would be able to uncover the traitors in their midst. Patiently, he went into himself and examined the healing he had started. It was almost done. Now was the time to test what little of his powers he could recall. When the wizards threatened his mind, his knowledge and his sense of self hid in the deepest part of his psyche. Now he began his journey through the newly healed tracts to find that knowledge.

As 'Quarl traveled cautiously, he felt a small tremor of fear. The deeper he went, the more intense the fear he felt. His body was flushed and covered with sweat. Like a wild animal, he could smell the stink of his own terror. 'Quarl stopped his journey and sought the source of this fear. He searched his own psyche thoroughly and was forced to conclude that the barrier in his mind was left by his enemies. The ones who would have mind-wiped him also left a warning system in his brain. If he removed the fear, or fought and defeated it, they would be alerted to what he was doing.

The Ah'Jarl examined his body. His people took good care of him. They made sure he was regularly exercised to keep his muscles strong. He knew, though, that he was not yet ready to challenge those who had done this to him. Neither his mind nor his body was recovered sufficiently, yet, to recover, he had to pass through that barrier of fear without triggering any alarms.

'Quarl decided that since he could neither remove the barrier nor fight it, he must surrender to it. He began his trip again, fixing in his soul the point that he must reach. No matter how afraid he became, when he ran, it must be forward, not back. He must let the fear itself take him where he wanted to be.

His screams, the sounds of a soul in torment, ripped through the palace. His people ran to his room, Asan reached over and touched the Ah'Jarl's head, then withdrew and stepped back.

"This must be. Put up your strongest shields around the room." he commanded.

The elders of the desert stood in a circle around their lord's bed and threw up a protective circle that blocked out all who would send or receive from the room.

The wizards on the other side felt the sudden stopping of information coming from the mage warrior and smiled in satisfaction. They reported the death of the desert warrior to their emperor.

The man on the bed felt the fear lessening and realized that he had help from somewhere, but it was not important where the help came from. He scanned quickly to make sure no additional damage was done to the newly healed areas of his mind, and went on with his quest.

The elders were tiring by the time his body relaxed. He had all the information he needed, but he must have time to study and sort what he had. 'Quarl felt the gentle touch of one of his elders and managed a smile for the man before he lost consciousness. The elders slowly lowered their shields, then sat on the floor of their lord's room, staring at him with worried eyes. When they were sure he was no longer in danger, they left the room and instructed the warriors guarding the Ah'Jarl's door to let none but their people enter.

*****

All'ya touched Mar'ya's arm and murmured, "It's time we left. Come."

"What, in the name of Crystal, is that?" Mar'ya pointed at the large animal tied to a post at the gate.

"It's a riding beast. You do know how to ride, don't you?" All'ya asked scornfully.

"I know how to ride, but I've never seen a riding beast this large before."

All'ya smiled and reached out to touch the animal's head. The creature responded by trying to bite her, stopping its efforts only when All'ya slapped it sharply on the nose. "This is Kal. Your beast is Jah. They are two of the finest battle steeds in all the desert."

Mar'ya wrinkled her nose, "I'll take your word for that." She stared dubiously at the long, spiked tongues and scaled tails of the two creatures.

"You can always walk." All'ya suggested.

Mar'ya sighed, "The thought of that long a walk is even more unattractive than Jah." She said as she mounted the bad-tempered steed.

Minutes later, two desert women left the city by a side gate. They rode slowly until they could no longer see the city, then they rode hard for another hour. As dawn broke over the horizon, they had put many miles between themselves and Crystal City.

"Those who will search for me will soon suspect that I'm bound for the desert. Though I planted a false trail earlier, it will prove easy for them to find that I'm not where I should be." Mar'ya said to her companion as they reined in the animals and dismounted.

All'ya shrugged, "Where we go, they won't find you. They have less power than you think."

"Do not underestimate the wizards, All'ya. See what they have done to your Ah'Jarl."

"They took him by surprise and treachery. That will not happen again. Come. We must walk a ways and let the animals rest. While we walk, I'll tell you the ways of our people and of the shielding.

"Our people are a race of warriors. We are proud of it." All'ya smiled, "You'll have no problem imitating the proud strutting of our people. What do you know of mind shields?"

"Nothing. My tutor, Wizard Barak, said that it was a waste of time as no power on our plane could hide its mind from the Wizard Council."

"You believed him?"

"I had no reason not to. Until yesterday, I would have sworn that he had no reason to lie to me."

"I'm sorry. I know the pain that comes when someone you trust betrays you. Listen and I will try to explain how shielding works. Every mind has a different feel. If you know a person well, the way Barak knew you, you can find that person's mind anywhere unless that mind is not there. Shielding hides your mind; it makes your mind not there."

"Then where is it?" Mar'ya frowned.

"Hidden. Concentrate on being a wild beast, know the beast, take on its feel, then, to the searchers, your mind is not there. Only a wild beast is there. I cannot teach you deep hiding, only surface camouflage."

"What good is that?"

"It will work well enough to get us to our destination. From what you say, the wizards are very sure that no one can hide from them. They will not look deeply for your mind, only skim the surface. When they don't find you in one direction, they'll simply move the search to another place. By the time they suspect, we should be out of their reach."

"Does it have to be a wild animal?"

"No. Better choose something you are familiar with. If you can manage it, just be nothing. Strive for the perfect stillness of a breeze, a grain of sand, or a pool of still water; whatever you are comfortable with. Now, practice."

Mar'ya sighed, *my feet hurt from walking, and I know that I have at least four blisters on my heels. I do not understand why I have to show so much consideration for this foul smelling, bad-tempered beast that tries to bite me every time I get on or off its back. To top it all off, this All'ya person wants me to pretend that I am a grain of sand, or even worse a wild animal. By Crystal, that is too much.* She shook her head. *No. If this is what I have to do to reach my goals and protect my people, then I will do it. I will spend the rest of my life wearing soft slippers if I succeed in this quest.* She gritted her teeth and plodded on. *Nothing and no one will stand in my way,* she decided. *This is my destiny and if I have to become a blank-minded, hard-ened warrior woman of the sands, I will do so.*

Mar'ya winced, and saw a small smile cross All'ya's face. "Share the joke, I need something to take my mind off my feet."

"I was thinking of my conversation with the elders earlier this day." All'ya glanced slyly at the young queen.

"Why do I get the feeling I'm not going to find this funny?"

All'ya laughed, "If you must know, I objected to being the one to escort you to the desert."

"Why?"

"You're a woman of the city, and also a queen; one not used to washing her own body. I was sure that you'd be soft, and quite useless. I must admit that you've held up well so far, with hardly a word of complaint."

"I did actually say a lot, did you miss it?" Mar'ya wrinkled her nose, "Riding beasts."

All'ya laughed. Mar'ya grinned, "Here's some more: My feet hurt."

"Don't worry," All'ya soothed, "Soon you will be used to walking, and even running great distances. Just think; after your training in the desert, you'll no longer be so soft, and will make a fitting mate for our lord. He'll be very surprised when he meets you."

Mar'ya grinned briefly, then sobered, "You believe that he'll recover?"

All'ya stared at her in surprise, "Of course he'll recover. Do you think that your wizards can defeat him? Silly Mar'ya, don't worry about our lord, he will be fine."

Mar'ya frowned, "They're not my wizards." She murmured in protest. As far as the Ah'Jarl recovering, Mar'ya was not as sure of that as All'ya seemed to be, but she wasn't going to argue about it. She had a more important question on her mind, "All'ya, can you use the weapons you carry, or are they for show?"

"Mar'ya, we of the desert never carry weapons for show. I'm warrior trained and have fought many battles for the people. Why do you ask?" All'ya replied as they remounted the beasts.

"Would you teach me to use the weapons? I'd like to be able to defend myself if the need arises. I've never liked the thought of relying on others for my protection, but since my grandmother's time, it's forbidden for women to learn the arts of war in the city. I would change that law," Mar'ya ended grimly.

All'ya glanced at the other woman in surprise, and grinned. "Very well, I'll teach you, but it won't be easy, and you'll have to work hard. It could be very dangerous to half learn the skill of combat."

Mar'ya nodded and smiled at All'ya. "It's a deal. If you do a good job teaching me, when I become ruler of Crystia, I'll put you in charge of teaching any city woman who wishes to learn. Maybe I'll even make you Captain of the Queen's guard."

"Don't sell your crops before the harvest," All'ya said with a grin.

"How can I fail with you on my side, oh Mighty Warrior of the desert?" Mar'ya shouted, as they spurred their mounts for a short run.

Suddenly, the desert woman stiffened, threw her head back, and closed her eyes. "Now, Little Queen, your absence has been discovered. The search for you has begun. Put up your defenses and ride as you never rode before. We have four days' ride until we reach safety."

The two women rode swiftly and silently through the night, their faces grim, minds tightly locked against discovery. Mar'ya felt a touch of fear deep inside as she thought of what her half-brother would do to her if she was caught. She pushed the fear aside. *I have no intention of being caught. I will would ride this ugly desert animal into the ground and then run on my aching feel until my heart bursts before I will let my enemies catch me.* Determination made her face even harder, *I swear that never again will I run from foes. When I face them next, it will be on my own terms and my own ground. I am water, flowing deep under the surface of the sand, I am a river.* Her body flowed across the sand as smoothly as her mind flowed beneath it.

For two days they rode, stopping only to eat and grab a few moments of sleep. Mar'ya who was unused to such strenuous riding, usually had to be forced to eat even a few bites of food.

"You have to keep up your strength, Mar'ya. Here, drop your shields for a while, I will cover both of us while you rest."

The next morning, All'ya said, "There's still another two nights of hard riding ahead of us, and we don't need you too weak and sick to take up your studies. The wizards are still concentrating their search in the mountains of the north. You must eat. You are not used to this hard traveling. If you are tired, tell me; I will do what I can to help you."

"I'm fine. Let's keep going."

All'ya sighed, "I know I don't need to remind you that time is not on our side in this venture, but driving yourself into the ground will cost us more time than it will save us."

"I know. You are right, but I am too tired to really care. All I want is a hot bath and a warm bed." She would not be judged a weakling by these people, so, gritting her teeth, Mar'ya pushed herself far beyond what she once thought was her limit.

When the sun rose on the fourth day, they did not stop as usual. Mar'ya, who had managed to stay on her beast by instinct alone, opened her eyes and caught a brief glance of silver desert sand shining in the light of the rising sun.

She wondered when they made the transition from dry scrub to desert proper. She had been in a haze of exhaustion for days, not noticing a thing about the passing scenery. She closed her eyes quickly against the sand being kicked up by her animal's swift passage, and sighed; *I hope that the sand means the end of this ride is near. If I never see another riding beast in my life, I will be overjoyed,* Mar'ya thought grimly. *I feel as if my rear end has been permanently attached to this animal's back. It is a thoroughly unpleasant sensation. Will I ever have any feeling in my rump again?*

All'ya called out, "See ahead, the two stones? When we reach them, throw yourself off the animal, but do not stop. Do you hear me?"

Mar'ya heard, but she was not sure she understood. A quick glance at the other woman's face in the dawn's light made her close her eyes tightly.

"By Crystal, you desert maniac, I did not come all this way to commit suicide." Mar'ya shouted as she watched the stones come closer. Her whole body tensed in anticipation of pain. "You're joking; please tell me you are joking."

She barely heard All'ya shout "Now!" because Mar'ya was too busy chanting the prayer for the dead as she clenched her teeth and threw her body off the speeding animal's back.

Chapter Twelve

She felt nothing but the wind as it wrapped around her, causing her to float slowly down through a soft sea of darkness. Mar'ya smiled. She thought that death would be more painful. With a soft bump, she landed on the ground... ground?

Mar'ya opened one eye, then the other. Maybe she was not dead. Neat trick, that soft landing. She would have to ask All'ya how it was done. She sat up, looked around, shook her head, and looked again. There was no trace of the silver sands. Instead, tall trees and gently waving grass shone soft blue in the moonlight.

In the distance, she heard the sounds of a river, and nearer, the thunder of a waterfall.

"All'ya, where are we?"

"In a safe place. This is the heart of the desert, where you'll be staying for the first part of your training."

Mar'ya sat up. "All'ya, am I missing something? How did we get here? Where are the riding animals? Where the heck is here, and how do I get back home? Are we dead?"

All'ya laughed and turned her head, drawing Mar'ya's attention to the four people coming toward them.

"You have missed nothing that won't be covered by your training. The animals are safe, though I didn't think you cared. When the time comes you'll know how to get home, and where you are." All'ya pulled one of Mar'ya's braids, "We are not dead, Little Queen. Now, let us go and meet your new tutors."

Mar'ya stood, her pug nose tilted. In spite of the desert clothes and her tightly braided hair, Mar'ya looked every inch the royal woman waiting for homage to be paid her.

All'ya nudged her hard in the side. "Stop being 'Royal Lady'. Get your nose out of the air and try to look humble," she hissed.

Mar'ya glanced at the other woman and sighed, letting her stance relax a little. All'ya shrugged. They could do nothing to hide that Mar'ya was not one of them. True, the desert people were proud and walked tall, but the way Mar'ya carried herself, even when relaxed, showed her true heritage.

Four tall females, covered from head to foot in black cloaks, came up to Mar'ya and All'ya. Mar'ya stared at them curiously. There was no way to tell them apart. When one of them spoke, her voice was as dry as dust.

"Greetings Daughter of the Desert, is this the student we have awaited?" The question and the greeting had been addressed to All'ya and the queen bristled. She was not used to being ignored. All'ya gave Mar'ya a quick warning glance then bowed her head to the four women.

"Greetings, Priestess of the Moon, this is Mar'ya, your new pupil. I have been asked to teach her the art of combat, and therefore request that I be allowed to remain."

Mar'ya turned to look at the young swordswoman. It had never occurred to her that All'ya might not be able to stay with her.

"There is much arrogance in this one, Desert Daughter. It has been a long time since one of her line has come to us for training. We know who you are, Child of Crystal."

The speaker turned and looked directly at the young queen for the first time. "We know your destiny better than you do, for we told the young mage warrior to accept your offer of an alliance. It is fitting that you come to us for training. Let us go now and begin, for there is much you need to know, and not much time to learn it. Already, measures are being taken to make our people look guilty of your abduction and murder." The four turned as one and walked away, leaving the younger women to follow.

When Mar'ya entered the tent, the four old ones, sitting in a circle on the floor, nodded a greeting to her and motioned that she join them. "We will begin with a test. We must see how much you know. This will be the easy part, Daughter of Crystal." One of the old ones said.

It could have been hours or minutes that the five women sat in silence. Mar'ya had lost all track of time when a voice said, "It is done. You have been well trained in the basics. It will not take long to teach you what is needed. Did you know, Daughter, that at one time your Lady Crystal trained the women of the desert in magic? It was long ago, before even our time. She and our Lord Stone were lovers, until she betrayed him."

"I don't believe you." Mar'ya said flatly.

"What don't you believe? That our gods were lovers, or that your Lady betrayed our Lord?"

"I don't believe that the Lady ever betrayed anyone. I have studied her teachings. Honor is important to Crystal. She would not betray one she loved."

"Our Lord is chained deep in the earth, Little One, that is a fact. Your Lady was not where she said she would be. That too, is fact. She ran and hid afterward, in shame, so some believe. We don't know."

"Crystal would not do this thing. Look elsewhere for your traitor. She is innocent. Is this why your people mistrust me so? Do they see history repeating itself?"

"The thought was in our minds." The old ones agreed. "No, Daughter of Crystal, we no longer believe you will betray our Lord, for it was on our advice that the Ah'Jarl accepted your offer of a treaty. We think that an old riddle will be solved. Maybe, with faith, both our gods will be freed. Now, let us continue the lesson. You have proved to us that our judgment was correct. There is the potential for great loyalty in you."

After the interview with her new tutors, Mar'ya stumbled into a small tent. She was asleep before her body hit the small sleeping mat.

"Come on, Lazy. Get up. If you want to be a warrior, we have to get your training done early."

"All'ya, I just went to sleep, it's still dark outside, and I'm hungry."

All'ya was adamant, "It's morning. Come on get up. You can have breakfast later. First we run, then we practice with the sword. After that, you can fix yourself something to eat. Get dressed and let's go."

"All'ya, I can't cook." Mar'ya scrambled to her feet and pulled on the rough desert clothes she had been wearing since they left the city. "My clothes stink. They need to be washed."

"Well, that's even more you will have to learn." All'ya grinned maliciously, "Don't worry, we'll start out slow and only run about a mile today. By the time you return to your palace you'll be running five miles easily. I promise."

It seemed like days later when Mar'ya at last staggered into her tent. She stared blankly at the uncooked food laying on her table. "All'ya what do I do with this stuff?"

"Cook it."

"How? I can't even start a fire."

All'ya sighed, "I'll show you just this once how to start the fire. After that, you're on your own."

Mar'ya looked at the food, at the pot, and the pitcher of water. She frowned, then threw everything into the pot and set it over the fire. The results were barely edible, but she was hungry. Ignoring All'ya's disgusted expression, Mar'ya wolfed down her meal.

All'ya sighed and pointed to four small bags on the table, "Mar'ya, the food would taste better if you used a little of the spices in those bags."

Mar'ya glanced at the bags, "Spices?"

"They add flavor to the food." All'ya said then winced as Mar'ya took a small handful from each bag, dumped it into her bowl stirred once and continued eating.

"You are right, it does taste better." Mar'ya said around a mouthful, as All'ya, her face tinged with green, quickly left the tent.

Mar'ya joined All'ya about half hour later, her dirty bowl in her hands, "What do I do with this?"

The other woman shuddered, "Put it and the pot in this bucket of water for now. We will clean up after you meet your tutors." All'ya instructed.

When Mar'ya returned to her small tent later that day, All'ya was waiting for her, "More practice, nothing hard this time, just some hand-to-hand combat and a few pointers on how to move softly. Right now, a herd of riding animals makes less noise than you do." As they left the small tent, All'ya wrinkled her nose. "They also smell better. Later, I will have to teach you how to wash your clothes. Don't frown at me. This is something every warrior must know. You can't ambush your enemy if he can smell you a meter away."

Four hours later, Mar'ya had scrubbed her pot and bowl, and was following All'ya to the river, "I don't have any clean clothes to replace these, and I refuse to wear dirty clothes after I bathe."

"They won't be dirty, just wet, and I have a robe you can wear until they dry."

"You are enjoying this, aren't you?" Mar'ya scowled at All'ya's back.

All'ya's teeth gleamed whitely in the constant dusk of the hidden oasis, "Yes. There is the river. Undress and let us begin your lessons."

"You drink from the same source that you bathe?" Mar'ya wrinkled her nose.

"No. We have wells for drinking water; I will show you where they are on the way back to your tent. This is flowing water, so it wouldn't matter anyway. Now, see this flat rock? Wet your clothes in the river, lay them out one piece at a time on the rock, then take a handful of the soap sand and rub it into the cloth. Use one of the smaller rocks to beat the dirt out, then rinse well in the river." All'ya watched as Mar'ya followed her instructions, and nodded. "Well done. Wring the water out and spread the clothes on that low bush while we bathe."

Mar'ya needed no second invitation to dive into the river. She watched closely as All'ya used the soap sand to wash her hair and body, then followed suit. "I wish my hair was as short as yours, will you cut it for me?"

All'ya shook the water out of her short, red hair, studied Mar'ya's thick, black, waist- length mane and shook her head, "No, but I will help you get the tangles out and show you how to braid it."

A tired, but clean young queen walked slowly back to her tent carrying an armful of damp clothes to be hung up in her tent. She barely had the energy to nod when All'ya pointed out the well and told her how to draw water for drinking and cooking.

That day set the pace Mar'ya followed for the next month. The first week, Mar'ya thought she would die as muscles, unused to exertion of any kind, screamed in protest. She was also sure she would starve to death. Mar'ya wished that she had learned to cook when she was younger. Her one meal a day, poorly prepared and barely edible, did little to sustain her.

After the first month, her cooking improved as she finally figured out how much spice to use and that it tasted better if she cooked the food with the spices, instead of adding them later. Her muscles ached less and she had more energy, but as soon as she began to relax, All'ya intensified her training schedule.

By the end of three months, she was sleeping only four hours a night, and every waking moment was spent in training of one kind or another. Nothing she did seemed to please her tutors, and anyone less determined would have given up. She chose this course because she had no choice; now, she stuck with it because she could not admit that a daughter of Crystal had been bested by the people of the desert. She clenched her fists, and did whatever was demanded of her.

Her reward was in the knowledge that her body, which had once been soft and useless for any purpose other than decoration, was now sleek and hard. She could run three miles without breathing hard, and defend herself with or without weapons. She was no great swordswoman or expert in hand-to-hand fighting, but All'ya taught her a few dirty tricks that might one day save her life. She knew that she would continue working with All'ya just for the sheer joy and freedom that the lessons gave her. One day, she swore, she would be better than the other woman.

Her training in magic was another story. She had spent two years in House Frya, and Shen's mother trained her well in the basics. Also, she was old enough that her powers were almost at full strength. All she needed was the discipline and the knowledge of how to channel the forces at her command. That part of her training was easy compared to physical.

Mar'ya spent less time studying with the speakers of Stone, and more time on weapons, and exploring the place she was in. Mar'ya took long walks, relishing the time spent alone. The soft, blue grass and sweet streams enchanted her. She found it hard to believe she had ever been too tired to pay attention to the scenery. When she first ran this trail, she concentrated on putting one foot in front of the other without falling flat on her face. Now, she ran around the area with an easy, loping gait, and enjoyed the peacefulness of this other place; a place that was not quite a part of her world. Once, she wondered where they were. Now, such thoughts did not bother her. She knew, and she also knew that if the need ever arose she could find her way back and be welcome. This small piece of another dimension was placed here by the desert mages hundreds of years ago. It was their place of refuge where they went when they needed renewal in body and soul. No wonder the Council of Wizards could not trace her. They underestimated the power of these desert people and did not suspect such a place existed.

That last thought brought the young queen up short, and she went to find her tutors. She still could not tell them apart, but she had learned to respect their knowledge.

"Mistress, I have a request to make of you. Take from me the secret of this place. There are those who would destroy it if they knew of its existence. I don't know what constraints have been put upon me by the Wizard Council, but I fear they may have some means to remove this thought from my mind."

Soft laughter greeted her statement, and one of the women said gently. "Relax, Little One. No man can take from your mind what you have learned here. The Council of Wizards think women are of no importance, so they have none who can read you now. What constraints they put upon you to hinder your development have been removed. What we have taught you is the very power of the Crystal Lady herself. Only women may know her full powers. All that we could, we have given you. Have confidence in yourself and in your knowledge. Now, it is time for you to leave us and continue your training with others. May the Lady of Crystal travel with you, Young Witch."

The four stood, and left the tent. The air around Mar'ya shimmered, and she found herself back in the desert sitting between two large rocks. The two riding animals stood quietly not far away, and All'ya lay sleeping on the ground to her right. Mar'ya reached out with her feet and prodded the sleeping woman in her side.

"Wake up, Lazy, we are out of sanctuary and have to return to my city."

"Not yet. You still have at least two more months of training to go. Go on, get some sleep. We are not going anywhere for a while. We have to wait for your guides."

Mar'ya grinned as she wrapped the sand-colored cloak of the desert people tightly around her body to ward off the chill of the night. She had not slept much in the last few months. One of the things she had learned, however, was to sleep wherever and whenever she had the chance. Stretching out next to All'ya, she fell asleep.

Early the next morning, the women were awakened by the sound of movement nearby. They opened their eyes to see a group of desert riders milling around them. The men were wild looking; their bright, red hair and beards flying untamed in the hot desert air. They handled their six-legged riding beasts with an ease that Mar'ya envied, using only the muscles in their powerful legs to keep the animals under control. She wondered briefly if her Champion had once been one like these, then shrugged the thought off.

"You keep a good watch, swordswoman. If we had been enemies, we would have murdered you in your sleep," one of the men teased. "We have come for the little one. Her training will now be in the hands of our masters." The speaker laughed, "Don't worry, we'll return her to you, unharmed, in two months if she lasts that long. We'll take good care of your soft, little queen."

All'ya rubbed her eyes and looked at the men for a long moment; she stretched and said with a smile, "This one may surprise you. There is pure desert steel in her."

All'ya stood up and reached for her weapons, then added softly, "Make sure she practices with her weapons, and also without. It is needful that she does not stint on her training with the physical, to concentrate solely on the arcane."

"This, we will do with joy." The man grinned fiercely, showing white teeth in his brown face. He turned to Mar'ya, "Come, Little Witch, we ride. We'll make you a true desert woman and a fitting mate for our lord before your training is over."

Mar'ya glanced at All'ya, unsure of whether she wanted to go on alone with these wild riders or not. The other woman nodded to her with a smile. "Go with them, Mar'ya, it is necessary for your training. I'll be waiting for you." She added, "Mayhap, they'll have the latest news of your city for you."

Mar'ya and Jah eyed each other with distaste. Jah tried to bite her as she mounted and earned himself a blow to the nose that rocked his head back. The riders watched with growing respect as Mar'ya climbed on the steed's back and indicated she was ready.

"What news do you have from Crystal City?" Mar'ya asked.

"Houses Mar, Kel, Capra, Frya, Tau, Sa, Orin, Sua, and the four Merchant Houses in the city, still support you. Supported by the desert people, your councilor Shen, House Mar and House Kel have closed the city's gates to wait for your return."

Mar'ya sighed. *Over fifty percent, thirteen of my Noble Houses have gone over to my half-brother's side. Well, that was about right. I suspected for quite a while that many of those lords would have been happier with a man ruling over them. The twelve houses that remained faithful all had women of power in them. Now I know why the wizards would not train my women. They find it much easier to manipulate and control men. At least one House in each of the outer districts has stayed loyal to me. I was lucky. It could have been worse. At least I have the comfort of knowing that I choose wisely in leaving Shen as my voice in the city.*

*****

The Wizard Council proclaimed Mar'ya dead, as they could find no trace of her anywhere on the planet. They also declared the desert tribes outlaws, saying they were responsible for the young queen's death. Of the twenty-five houses of Crystal, thirteen supported the usurper. They left the city and took their large, private armies with them. They hoped their leaving would so demoralize the remaining Houses that the city would fall easily, for they had all been promised much power and riches by the foreign emperor and the Wizard Council.

The other twelve Houses remained faithful. With the help of the city guard and the desert tribesmen, they declared Crystal City and palace closed to the emperor and his followers. When Emperor Gregor appealed to the Crystal Guardians, they quoted the prophecy of the old ones,

"The Crystal City must be ruled by a woman of power or be destroyed."

Emperor Gregor gathered his army together and laid siege to the city. After a few minor skirmishes, the tribesmen won the right of their women to visit the river daily to do washing, but the women were carefully searched, both when they departed the city and when they returned.

Inside the city, a council of war was held; Asan looked around the council table and pushed the sheet of paper forward. "Here. This is an addendum to the original agreement. It spells out, in detail, the rights and privileges of the Ah'Jarl."

Shen frowned, "Could this not wait until our queen returns, or at least until your Ah'Jarl awakens? Up until now, we have worked well together. Things are going well. There is no reason to change an agreement approved by our Crystal Guardians and your Speakers."

Asan scowled, "The original agreement was just an outline. We demand that there be more detail before we continue working with your people."

Shen sighed, "Then we sit and wait until your Ah'Jarl and our queen are present. This agreement affects them more than it does us. It is their place to make any changes, not ours." The other House Lords nodded their agreement.

"Then my people leave at dawn tomorrow, taking the Ah'Jarl with us." Asan stated flatly.

Shen's head snapped back as if he had been slapped. "It is as I expected, but I am sure you will be able to explain to the crystal witch what you have done when she returns. Or maybe you do not expect her to return?" He reached across the table, not even bothering to read the paper he signed, and threw it at Asan, "You and yours, stay away from me and mine." He snarled, walking out of the council chamber. There was a moment of stunned silence, then the other House Lords stood and left as well.

"That was not well done, Asan," 'Ulan's voice was mild.

"I saw her heart. Would you defend her? Maybe you encouraged her to choose you and betray our Ah'Jarl?"

"I am 'Ulan, chief of the Northern Desert Tribe. I am sworn to the Speakers, and through them, to the Ah'Jarl. You, Asan, would try to shame me, but I say the shame is yours. Do as you will. On your head will the wrath of the

Speakers fall. I will stand by the city until the Speakers and the Ah'Jarl release me."

'Ulan walked out of the room. When he saw Shen and the House Lords standing in the castle foyer, he joined them. "Shen, I swore to your queen that I would aid you in securing her city. I will not be forsworn. My people from the north stand beside you, no matter what you decide to do."

Shen studied the nomad, then nodded, "We will wait until our queen returns. She will return won't she?" He asked, a worried look on his face.

'Ulan nodded, "She will return, the swordswoman guiding her is the best in the desert, and my betrothed. All'ya will keep her safe."

"Then we wait." Shen smiled briefly at 'Ulan and walked away.

Chapter Thirteen

The Ah'Jarl arose from his bed, dressed and went out to see what was going on in the city. For ten weeks, he had done nothing but eat and sleep, while his mind healed, and his memories returned. Now, he was ready to fulfill his side of the bargain with Crystia.

There was great rejoicing among his own people when he strode out of the palace with all his wits restored. The people of the city reserved their judgment. True, he was their queen's Champion, but they knew nothing of him.

The warrior, after meeting with the council, went to the city walls, accompanied by one of his people and looked down on the besieging army.

"Those are the ones that tried to destroy me. When the time comes, I will not be gentle with them. I will grind them and their weapons into the dust and their memory will be blown away by the desert wind. This, I swear, on Stone." His voice shook with suppressed anger.

"My Lord, that is not a thing you can do alone. According to the prophecy you will need the young queen's aid. Only together, can you have your revenge." The Nomad Elder warned.

'Quarl sighed, "Are you sure that Queen Mar'ya is safe?"

"Yes. Our last report says she is doing well in her studies and should be on her way back to the city in another month." Asan replied, not meeting the Ah'Jarl's eyes.

'Quarl wondered briefly about the man's discomfort, then dismissed the thought. Living behind walls was not something his people were used to.

"I hope it is soon enough to save her country. The heart of these people is with her. Look at them. Every day they line the walls, watching for her return." 'Quarl shook his head, took a deep breath, and led the elder down from the walls of Crystal City.

The Ah'Jarl and the desert warriors drilled and trained the city's guards. They practiced with the armies of the twelve remaining Houses until they all fought as one unit and among the armies and their leaders there was no dissension.

He noticed that the Northern Desert Tribe worked best with the city troops. They were like a family. It puzzled him how well they got along compared to the restraint between his elders and the elders of the ruling Houses of Crystia. However, he had a lot on his mind. He trusted his people, and did not question them. He turned his mind to the supplies in the besieged city, and how to keep the spirits of the people within the walls high.

Each night, he sent small raiding parties out of the city to raid the encampments of his enemies, while the desert elders, the Named Guardians, and he battled the Wizard Council to provide protection for the raiders. Gradually, he took the reins of the city in his hands, and none questioned his right to do so.

Their queen named him Champion, and even though they didn't completely trust him, he proved himself a leader of great cunning and strength.

*****

"Rowan, where is she? It's been three months. Why does she not come home?"

"Shen, she is safe and well. That much we do know. It was necessary that she leave Crystal City. Now, tell me what really troubles you?"

"My sister, you know what worries me. Two weeks ago, we were able to work in harmony with the desert elders; our troops made successful raids on the enemy camp, and we cleaned out most of the traitors put in place by that old snake Barak. Now, however, things have changed. The city is tearing itself apart over the new treaty."

"What is this? I have heard nothing of a new treaty." Rowan frowned

"The Desert Eldest, Asan, told us in the last council meeting a month and a half ago, that they were unhappy with the original treaty. If we did not agree to certain changes, they would withdraw all support from Crystal City. I don't even know what the damned thing said. I was so angry, I just signed the papers and threw them back at him. If Mar'ya does not return soon, I fear that, between the desert people, their Ah'

Jarl, and the enemy, there will be nothing left for her to come back to."

"Ah, Shen, do not blame the Ah'Jarl. I don't believe he knows what his people are up to." Rowan, Keeper of Crystal's hair, and Shen's younger sister, sighed. "As for the rest, I think you are correct. If only this Ah'Jarl would show himself, maybe he could pull our people together and help us hold on until the queen returns. If he cannot do this thing, then I fear Crystal City will be lost."

"What about the Guardians? Will they help?"

Rowan shook her head, "They will not interfere. Emperor Gregor has petitioned them to name him king, but they refuse. They say the queen is still alive, and even if she was not, the prophecy that Crystal City has to be ruled by a woman must be followed."

Shen shrugged, "If they don't name him king, then it's likely the city will be destroyed anyway." He turned to his sister with a grim smile, "If Mar'ya does not return, that will make you the next queen of Crystia."

"No thank you, Brother, Dear. I don't want the job. We have already lost thirteen Houses to the enemy."

"The women of power would support you."

"Yes, but Mar'ya is the only one with the strength and the power to defeat the wizards."

"Rowan, do you really think she can do it?"

"Oh yes, Big Brother. Do not underestimate the strength of House Sultav Witches. She will be able to do anything she sets her mind to."

"Our little sister has turned out to be quite a woman hasn't she?" Shen said softly.

Rowan chuckled softly, "Yes. Our father and her mother would be very proud of her. Have you told her?"

"No. Maybe someday, when the time is right. Now, there are too many things that she must deal with."

"I would think she would be pleased to know that her true father did not betray her. Did Richard suspect?"

"Yes, the old goat knew. That's why he sent me to Mar'ya's room on her sixteenth birthday."

Rowan stared at Shen in shock, "Crystal and Stone, I hate that custom. It is something only the western barbarians would think of. What did you do?"

"What could I do? Thank heavens Mar'ya was not willing to play that game. We bargained, and the result is that Mar'ya now believes I don't like women." Shen shook his head sadly. "The things I do for my sisters."

Rowan giggled, "She thinks you don't like women? Are we talking about Shen, House Frya, also known as the 'staff of the mountains'?"

"Rowan, don't be vulgar." Shen blushed. "Where did you hear that phrase anyway?"

Rowan shrugged, "It doesn't matter. Shen, I think we should tell her the truth."

"After this is over. I wish that I was more like our father. Maybe if I had paid more attention to our weapons master when I was young, I would be able to help Mar'ya now. I feel so helpless being trapped in the city like this. I wish we could get our ships out of the harbor. Maybe get some of our people out of the city."

"Peace, Shen. What good would our small merchant ships do against the mighty warships of the western kingdom? They are better at war than we are. To our people, a battle is two men with swords, each fighting for the honor of his House or his tribe. To those western men, war is an art form. Look at all the weapons they have arrayed out there. I don't know why they have not moved against us in force before now, but I'm glad they haven't. The longer they wait, the better chance we have of the queen returning or the Ah'Jarl awakening. Magic is the only force that can save us from defeat." Rowan giggled again, "We are not completely locked into the city, you could disguise yourself as one of the desert women and go out to the river to do your wash." She gently teased her brother.

Shen grinned and slipped his arms around his sister and gave her a brief hug as the two returned to their silent watch.

*****

Emperor Gregor, Lord of all the Western Lands, was a huge man with black hair and piercing blue eyes. He was a leader who commanded the respect and love of all his subjects.

He sat in his command tent and scowled at the black-robed wizards facing him, "I do not like being lied to by my allies, and all the reports that I received from the Crystal Palace point to the fact that you wizards have lied to me. My spy in the city tells me that the desert warrior still lives. I made a serious mistake in sending him back to my sister. It was a spiteful deed, and I should have learnt a long time ago that a ruler should be above such behavior."

The emperor shook his head and continued, "You wizards have been encouraging all the flaws in my character; I wonder why. Does it make it easier for you to control me?"

Bunji, Chief of the Wizard Council, ignored the emperor's last statement. "Sire, it is impossible for the warrior to still be alive. We felt his death."

"Really?" Gregor raised one eyebrow.

"We think the desert people are using an imposter, Sire."

"You think? What happened to all your vaunted powers? Can none of give me any definite facts?"

"We cannot read the minds of the desert folk, Emperor Gregor."

Gregor closed his eyes. He felt a headache starting, "Why not?"

"We don't know. In all the centuries we have worked in this land, never have we been able to read them."

"So the desert warrior could be alive and well?"

"No, My Lord. When we destroyed his mind, we created a link that only death could break. The warrior is dead."

The Emperor nodded, "I hope so. For all our sakes, I hope so. Your council and my father came up with this plot. I'll fight your war for you, but don't let arrogance blind you to the fact that these desert folk may have a stronger magic than your own. I'll not have my troops destroyed because you made a mistake. Do you understand me, Wizard?"

The wizards stood, and Bunji turned to the emperor, "Are you threatening us, Lord Gregor? This is a land that stands against the very foundation of your own power. How long will your rule last if the women in your kingdom decide to follow the path of these crystal witches? For over a hundred years, the Wizard Council has worked to remove this abomination from our world and give the power of rule and magic into the hands of those fitted to wield it. Women should never have power of any sort. We of the Wizard Council have much more to lose in this struggle than you do. We will not fail. We cannot fail."

"You will only lose some of your power, I will lose the lives of men who trust me. Do not compare the two. So, where is the queen, and why don't the Crystal Guardians declare me king of this land?"

"Sire, we have warned you. Do not try to manipulate the Crystal Guardians. They will not involve themselves in any way with this struggle. They serve only Crystal and her prophecy. They will not oppose you if you win, for they will see that as Crystal's wish. However, they know where the queen is, they are in constant contact with Crystal..."

"Where is my sister? You never did say."

"Rumors have it the witch is in the mountains in the north, somewhere in the caves of House Frya where a part of Crystal rests."

"Rumors, Bunji?"

"Aye Lord, rumors. Since Barak was killed, we have received no reliable information. The Wizard Council is not yet ready to challenge

Crystal herself. When the time is right, we will destroy her."

"When will that be?"

"Our timetable does not concern you, Emperor of the Western Lands. The Crystal Goddess is our business, not yours."

Emperor Gregor frowned thoughtfully as the wizards turned and walked out of his tent. For a long moment, he sat alone, then called for his captain of the guards.

"Dealing with these wizards gives me a headache," he snarled. "Charles, how goes the siege of Crystal City? Is there any indication that they may be ready to surrender?"

"The siege goes well, my Emperor. At least those damned night raids by the city troops have stopped. I have the feeling that things aren't working out too well between the city folk and the desert rats. What with the queen not being there and the desert blaming the city folk for what happened to their Ah'Jarl, it's just a matter of waiting."

"She chose a bad time to leave her city." Gregor rubbed his clean shaven chin. "I wonder what she is up to?"

"No telling with women, my Emperor. It's good for us she left when she did, even better she left the rats in charge. More than half her noble families came over to our side." Charles shrugged, "Any woman who would prefer to deal with those savages from the desert instead of us is strange anyhow."

Emperor Gregor laughed, then winced as the pain in his head intensified. "Ahh, and we are so civilized, aren't we? We leave our country and come uninvited to this one. We tell the ruler that she must turn her throne over to us or we will completely destroy her and hers. No, Charles, she made the only decision she could. Crystia and the Stoneland Desert share this land. We are the common enemy." He glanced at his captain's puzzled face and waved his hand.

"Never mind, Charles, it's just that I have a bad feeling that we all, even our mighty wizards, are under-estimating my little half-sister. Double the patrol outside the city gates. Pay special attention to the desert women as they go to and from the river. Make very sure that my half-sister does not enter Crystal City. I want her captured and brought to me. Also, inform me immediately if you hear rumors of any problems in the city that we may be able to capitalize on."

Charles grinned and saluted smartly, "As you command, Sire."

Emperor Gregor watched his man leave and stared at his desk. "What am I doing here? I already have more power, land, and wealth than I can control. Yet here I am, playing puppet to the Wizard Council and my dead father's wishes. It doesn't bother me that women rule the land of Crystia. They are doing a good job. Their people seem to be happy for the most part." He spoke aloud in the empty tent.

Gregor rubbed his eyes. The pain in his head was now making him sick to his stomach, and he staggered as he stood up. "All this pain, just so the wizards can keep me under control. Damn them and their dark god to the deepest pits of Taron." He muttered, and gasped as the pain drove him to his knees. He grabbed a handful of his hair and pulled hard, tearing it from his scalp. "I will fight their battle for them," he wiped the blood from his wounded head with an impatient hand, "When we have won, I will take my men back across the sea, and leave the wizards to worry about what happens next."

As Gregor tried to pull himself up, his bloody hand slipped on the edge of the desk, slamming his lower body into the corner. He cried out and crumpled to the floor. The guard outside his tent rushed in, "My Lord Emperor, what has happened?"

"Charles, send him to me, at once."

"Yes, my Lord." The young soldier ran out of the tent and, a few minutes later, Charles entered.

"Charles, listen to me," Gregor groaned, ignoring the pain. "Something is going wrong. The wizards are worried. There is too much that they do not know about these people. I have a feeling..." He stopped, and his whole body shuddered with pain, "Find a way to move our people close to the beach. Tell them... be prepared to get on the ships at a moment's notice, forget the equipment... things can be replaced but their lives cannot."

"My Lord, you need a doctor. We can discuss this later." Charles frowned.

"Charles, put the traitors on the front lines... move our people back." Gregor grabbed the other man's hand. "Do this now!"

"I will obey you. Now let me go, and I will get a doctor for you." Charles stopped as he reached the entrance of the tent, "My Emperor, what do I tell the wizards if they question me?"

Gregor closed his eyes, "Strategy... tactics... whatever..."

When the doctor arrived Gregor was still on the floor, "My Lord Emperor, what happened to you?"

Gregor gave a strangled laugh, "I unmanned myself, then fell, knocked my head."

The doctor examined Gregor's head, "My lord…"

Gregor stared into the man's worried eyes, "It is as I said."

The doctor returned the look, nodded, and began cleaning and bandaging Gregor's torn scalp.

"Doctor, we are the barbarians here. Look at that strange and wondrous city glistening in the sun. So beautiful; something that most mortals see only their dreams." Gregor winced, "A symphony of light and shadow. I wonder and marvel at the skill of the builders who created such soft, flowing beauty of hard rock, and sharp angles. We are going to destroy that dream, shatter the stones, and leave the people homeless. This is not how the empire makes war."

The doctor snorted, "All war is barbaric, Lord Gregor. Now hold still while I bandage your head."

"I pity my poor half-sister, trapped in a deadly web spun by our father and the Wizard Council."

"My Lord, be still." The doctor glanced nervously around the empty tent. "Guards," he called. When one of the men looked inside, the doctor beckoned him over, "Come and help me move the emperor to his bed."

The two men lifted Gregor and gently laid him on his bed. The doctor waved the other man out of the room and turned to his patient.

"Let's see if your original diagnosis was correct, Lord Gregor."

Gregor winced as the doctor removed his trousers and examined him, "Well, good news, Your Highness. You will be able to father another generation of emperors, but it was close.

You must be more careful wandering around this small tent." The doctor sighed, picked up the soiled cleaning cloths and stood, "Lord Gregor, try to get some sleep. You are going to be very sore for a while, and walking will be painful. Would you like me to give you something to help you sleep?"

Gregor shook his head. He was already asleep when the doctor left the tent.

Chapter Fourteen

Her guides would answer none of her questions concerning her Champion. Either they did not know how he fared, or they were under orders not to tell her anything. Mar'ya had much to occupy her thoughts, and the ride was a short one to a small cave formed in the heart of a large sand hill. There, the riders dismounted and led her inside. After ten minutes, Mar'ya realized that this was another of those otherworld places created by the desert mages. In the heart of the sand, the second phase of her training began.

For three more months she learned the magic of the desert warriors. Mar'ya was disappointed when she realized that they were only teaching her the basics. She found their discipline fascinating, and would have liked to learn more.

"I wish to know more warrior magic. Can I come back and study with you when this is all over?" She asked her tutors.

"Are you not betrothed to the Ah'Jarl? He'll supply the rest of the knowledge. You have the magic of Crystal, and some of the warrior's magic. The lord has the warrior's magic and some Crystal magic. So together, you form a whole. This is as it should be."

"Then the mage warrior has recovered?" she asked eagerly.

"We have heard nothing," she was told, and no amount of further questioning got her additional information. They still did not trust her where their lord was concerned.

This phase was more rigorous physically, but easier mentally. The men worked her hard with weapons, showing her how to fight from the back of the large battle steeds, and she grew to respect Jah's skill at biting his unsuspecting opponents.

Each morning, the riders took her out with them, teaching her the ways of the desert, showing her how to find life in the sands she always considered lifeless. They taught her how to read tracks, find water, and create shelter from the wild storms that wreaked havoc and changed landmarks. They taught her to be comfortable in her environment, and to survive without servants or silk sheets. They taught her how to fight without weapons, and showed her ways to use a larger opponent's size against him.

Gradually, she gained the respect of these hardened desert warriors. Every night, she went to bed tired in both mind and body and counted her bruises. Mar'ya was surprised to discover that there were still new muscles left to ache. She thought all of them had been discovered in the women's retreat. Now, she knew better.

She learned exercises of mind and body that were designed to create a harmonious whole. Instead of manipulating the outer forces as one did in Crystal magic, the warriors used their inner resources. They taught her to travel the secret parts of her mind and disguise her thoughts from within instead of using the Crystal force to camouflage herself.

One day, Mar'ya was practicing riding Jah without using the reins when she heard another rider approaching her at full speed.

"Ho, Little Witch, defend yourself!" The huge rider shouted.

Mar'ya grinned. There was no way she could best this man on Jah's back. He held his curved sword in both hands. She needed both hands to stay on Jah's back. Well, if she could not beat him fairly, she would have to cheat.

She freed her own sword and laid it across her knees. Then, she and Jah waited for the rider to reach them. At the last moment, she turned Jah, avoiding the sword, and opening the other beast's flank for a vicious bite from her own steed. Jah took the opportunity to use his massive tail to knock the front two legs of the other animal out from under him. In the confusion, Mar'ya slapped the man smartly across the back of his shoulders with her sword, then rode out of reach.

"So, Little One, you think you have bested the greatest warrior in the desert, do you?" The man laughed, and Mar'ya recognized the huge red-haired man as Karl.

"No, Karl. My Lord 'Quarl is the greatest warrior in the desert."

Karl dismounted, still laughing, "He's not here. He is in your city, and that makes me the greatest warrior in the desert."

Mar'ya joined his laughter, "No, that makes Jah the greatest warrior in the desert." Jah approved this statement by throwing back his head and screaming a challenge across the sand.

"So dismount. Put away your sword and let me see how well you do without your mighty hero."

Mar'ya slid to the sand, and stepped away from Jah. As Karl rushed her, she heard All'ya's voice in her mind, 'legs, hip, shoulder.' Mar'ya braced herself and was more surprised than Karl when she actually succeeded in throwing him to the ground.

Karl, lay on his back, a huge grin on his face, "Yah, you'll do. We of the desert are truly wonderful. We have taken a soft, little witch and created the beginnings of a good warrior. You must continue to practice, build up your strength. Then, one day you can return to the desert and challenge me fairly."

Mar'ya threw herself on the sand next to him. She liked this large, gentle nomad warrior. He reminded her of Alex, "Does this mean I am ready to return to my city?"

"So eager to leave us, Little One?"

"My people need me." Mar'ya glanced at him, "And quit calling me little. I'm quite tall for a woman of my people."

Karl laughed, "True, but you are small for a woman of my people." He stood and pulled her up. "Come. It is time you left us. We have taught you more than we should have already."

Mar'ya gave a sigh, "I guess that I'll just have to use my feminine wiles to convince the Ah'Jarl to teach me more." She flirted gently.

Karl's laughter rang across the desert, "Mar'ya, you are truly a daughter of the sand. I've no doubt that you'll try, and most likely you'll succeed." Then he added, with a smug look, as she prepared to ride off, "Just be careful the Lord does not use his masculine wiles to get you to teach him more of your Crystal magic."

*****

One night, about five-and-a-half months after Mar'ya left the city, Shen came to see 'Quarl in his room. "I'm worried about our queen and the morale of our people."

The Ah'Jarl glanced up from the charts he was studying, "Lord Shen, tell your people to have patience. They might also try to cooperate with my tribesmen in defending the city." 'Quarl snapped.

Shen stiffened, "Warrior, you claim to be a master of the magic arts, can you not find our queen and call her home? Her people need her."

"Noble Shen, my people tell me that your queen is safe. It has been five months since she has left, and we can hold out for a while longer. Tell your people not to worry, I have given my word that I would protect her people as I would my own, and I will not be forsworn." 'Quarl spoke shortly to Shen, for he had other things on his mind at the time.

"Lord, be careful. My cousin has been betrayed many times in her young life. It would destroy any chance of peace between our people if she returned and found that the one she named Chosen above all others had betrayed her."

The Ah'Jarl frowned, "Why do you see betrayal of your queen around every corner? I will not betray her. All that I have done was in the best interest of this city."

Shen bowed, "I hope, my Lord, that she agrees with you upon her return."

Shen turned away and did not tell him of the treaty the desert elders had forced him to sign.

Among themselves, the House Lords of Crystia worried, and watched all the Mage Warrior did closely. They began to question his every order, and the city came to a standstill. The armies of Crystia no longer drilled with the desert warriors, the raids stopped, and the Named Crystal Guardians refused to blend their minds with those of the desert people.

The Ah'Jarl was angry and frustrated, but he never questioned his people, blaming it all on the stiff-necked pride of the city dwellers and their witches.

*****

At last, word came. The queen was on her way home. Crystal herself notified the Crystal Guardians in the city. The hot desert breezes brought the message to the elders of the tribes. There was great joy among both peoples, for the desert elders did not really wish the queen harm. Asan had seen within her heart, and did not trust her, but they hoped the new treaty would give their Ah'Jarl more power to restrain her. They were nervous of the consequences; not of what they had done, but of the methods they used.

Their lord would be angry when he found out, but would understand and forgive them. In spite of this belief, none of them were eager to tell their Ah'Jarl what actions they had taken on his behalf while he still slept. So, they said nothing and hoped the young queen would accept the new treaty without comment. They did not know about the queen's temper. The city elders, who were well acquainted with her temper, crossed their fingers and hoped that she would place the blame on the desert tribesmen where it belonged, and not on them.

The warrior mage knew nothing of all this. He only knew that the leaders of the city questioned his every order. He was frustrated, and swore that when the arrogant, young queen returned, he would have much to say about the behavior of her people; people so proud they would risk the safety of their land for petty spite.

*****

As she traveled with her escort to the place where All'ya waited, Mar'ya thought about what Karl had said. *I have never thought of the mage warrior as a man. To me, he was always just a means to an end; the defeat of the westerners and the safety of my people. I never thought beyond the end of the war. I never thought about the intimacies that our agreement called for.* She shook her head. *I still cannot see the mage warrior as my husband and lover. All my memories of him involve the ugly, drooling, hulk of scarred, idiot child I left behind at my castle. I have no idea what he really looks like or what his character is like.* Mar'ya frowned, *Does he have some pretty desert woman who will make him regret the demands of our agreement? If he does, will he be faithful to his first love, and insist that she come to city and be his lover, or will he stand by his word and be true lover and husband to me?*

No matter how hard I try, all I can see is a small blond boy, with crossed eyes. Who is he, and why does he keep haunting me? She smiled at the memory. For a brief moment, she was an innocent, young woman, free and not encumbered with all the titles of her birth.

She sobered, once again a queen. Thoughts of a husband or lover were for the future. The important thing was to get back to her city, to defeat her half-brother, and to do some rearranging of the wealth in her country. Her personal life would have to be placed on indefinite hold until she had her public life under control.

The riders took her to a small desert village where All'ya waited for her. The two women rested there for a day, gathering supplies and renewing their friendship. Mar'ya waited until she saw All'ya enjoying a still moment by the village well, then walked over and sat next to her. They were both quiet for a long while, watching the bustle around them before Mar'ya asked the question that was uppermost in her mind.

"All'ya what is the mage warrior really like? I mean, as a man." She felt her cheeks grow warm.

All'ya glanced at the Mar'ya in surprise then turned away to hide the grin on her face. "He's a mighty warrior. That's why you chose him as Champion is it not?"

"All'ya! That isn't what I mean, and you know it. Is there anyone else who has prior claim to his affections? Is he a gentle man or a rough warrior who knows naught of tenderness?"

"Why should you care if there was another love in his life? You have the Lord's word and he won't betray it. I know that he is good to children, and they all love him, so he'll be a good father to any children you may have. He has a sense of fun and laughter. He's not just a warrior, Mar'ya, he's also a man. The rest, you'll have to discover for yourself. I wonder why you didn't think of all these things before."

"It didn't seem important before now. Now, I'm beginning to believe that he might well recover to keep his part of our bargain, and I'm worried about what I may have gotten myself into."

"Think on the alternative, Mar'ya, then the choice of having a savage desert rat for mate will not seem so terrible." All'ya snarled. "You made a bargain. Now, it's too late for second thoughts. Don't be forsworn, Crystal Witch. We of the desert do not take kindly to those who will not keep their words."

Mar'ya felt tears spring to her eyes. How had her innocent questions become so misunderstood? "All'ya..." she began then stopped. *Why does it matter to me what this woman thinks? I will not beg forgiveness for a sin I did not commit.* Standing up and looking every inch the Holder of the Crystal Throne, Mar'ya walked away.

In the privacy of her tent, she let the doubts and tears surface. *This will be the last time I show weakness. I will begin to deal with others as they deal with me. I will never offer friendship again, I will never open myself to that pain again. How can I be a friend to those who will not take the time to know or understand me? Why does everyone assume the worst of me?*

The two women were silent as they started out the next morning. Mar'ya was nursing feelings of betrayal and All'ya was puzzling over the events of the night before. There was no explanation for what had happened. Mar'ya was behaving like a virgin bride about to be sacrificed.

"What know you of men?" All'ya asked suddenly. She had a ridiculous suspicion. Everyone knew of the city's customs: No woman of the city over sixteen was a virgin, and the queen was eight years past that age.

Mar'ya was silent. How could she answer that question without embarrassing herself by telling this woman of her shame? No, she could not do that.

"Mar'ya, in the desert, it's no shame for a woman to be a virgin on the night of her wedding. It's a highly prized thing."

"It is?" Mar'ya asked, her surprise causing her to speak. She bit her lip and added bitterly, "Well, your Lord is going to get a highly prized thing, though I doubt very much that large, drooling idiot will even realize it."

"Don't worry. Lord 'Quarl will not stay that way." All'ya smiled at her companion. "But I know your customs. How did this come to be?"

"My father chose Shen of House Frya, my cousin, as the man to visit me on my sixteenth birthday. I wasn't ready for a man's attention and bargained with Shen. I would make him my chief-councilor and give him great power at court if he would help me. So we made a bargain, and since Shen had no great desire to bed a woman, he was easily swayed. After that, of course, I didn't dare take a lover, even if I'd been tempted, for then, my secret would have been discovered, and both Shen and I humiliated."

All'ya smiled gently. "So that was behind your questions last night. I'm sorry I reacted the way I did, but you see, I didn't understand. Don't fear. Your secret is safe with me. I suggest that you tell the Ah'Jarl this thing before your wedding night. 'Twill go easier for you if you do. Mar'ya, you do like men, don't you? I mean you have no leanings to desire women?"

Mar'ya glanced at the other woman then smiled. "I don't know. To date I have desired neither man nor woman. Are you wed All'ya?"

"Don't you know? I'm betrothed to the northern chief 'Ulan, the young man you wanted to take instead of the mage warrior."

"I really wouldn't have done that, you know."

"Really?" All'ya asked dryly.

"Well, maybe I would have. I was desperate, any straw to anchor against the wind, swords-woman."

"Oh no. Don't you dare call my man a straw and add insult to injury." The women looked at each other and laughed.

The air was cleared between the two and they rode on. The trip back to the city was different from the one out. They used the early mornings to practice with their swords, and rode through the night, finding shelter and sleeping during the hottest hours of the day.

It was three days later when the city and the besieging army outside its gates came into view. The women dismounted and looked at each other in dismay.

"Do you have any ideas how we're going to get into the city?" All'ya asked softly.

"There's a way in, but we'll have to get under the gates." Mar'ya whispered. "Any idea how we can reach the walls without being seen?"

"You're the witch, can't you just magic us in?" All'ya asked with a grin. "Come. Let's find concealment and think this over. Maybe we can contact my people within the city and arrange for them to create a disturbance on the other side so we can sneak in."

Softly and slowly, they retraced their tracks until they were hidden from view by a group of large stones. Then, lying low, Mar'ya kept watch while All'ya tried to mentally contact the desert elders inside the city walls.

Chapter Fifteen

"Is this a private party, or can anybody join?" The voice came from a clump of bushes next to them.

"Alex. Oh Crystal, I have never been so glad to see anyone." Mar'ya rolled to her side and wrapped her arms around her cousin, burying her head on his chest.

Alex put his chin on her head and grinned at the scowling All'ya. "Relax, Nomad Swordswoman, I've been waiting for you for a week. Crystal told my wife that Mar'ya was on her way home." He tugged one of Mar'ya's braids. "It's a good thing I was here. You two have no sense. Anyone could have been here to ambush you."

"Are you going to get us into the city?" Mar'ya moved away from him.

"Hmm, that's the plan." Alex studied his young cousin carefully, "You look good." He said finally.

All'ya shook her head, "Who are you?" she demanded.

Mar'ya smiled happily, "This is my most beloved cousin, Alex." She whispered.

"I thought that was Shen." Alex teased.

"Shen is not here. How is he? How is the city, and how are my people?"

"Fine, intact and missing you."

Mar'ya sighed happily, "Okay, get us into the city."

Alex rolled onto his back and closed his eyes, "Wake me when it gets dark."

*****

'Quarl, stood on the walls of the west tower and looked down at the army that surrounded Crystal City. His anger and frustration were evident on his face, and the scar that ran from eyebrow to chin gleamed whitely in the moonlight, making him look even larger and more cruel than usual.

Down there are my enemies, and I wonder how much panic their loss of control over my mind caused them. Do they just think I am dead? He shrugged, *if they think that, they have gravely underestimated the strength of the desert magic. Will those western wizards ever learn not to scorn what they do not understand? Of course, I have been guilty of the same mistake; that of underestimating my foes. They captured me and almost destroyed me. If not for their arrogance in sending me to the castle to taunt the young queen, and thereby putting me in reach of my people, they might very well have succeeded. I will not forget what they tried to do, and swear they will pay dearly for it. I will have my revenge in spite of the stiff-necked pride of this cursed city.*

"Master, I'm sorry to interrupt, but the witch and All'ya should be reaching the city soon."

The tall warrior turned and looked at his tribesman with a scowl, then shook himself like an animal shedding water from his fur. "Tell me again the reason for sending the soft one into the strongholds of our people. How do we know that she can be trusted?"

"The elders decided that she needed the training. They have a responsibility to aid others of their kind whenever needed. She will not betray her training. That is a secret that is close to the heart of the Crystal Goddess herself. Also, the treaty stipulated that you will be at her side to ensure that she does not misuse her knowledge." The other added slyly.

"Ahh yes, the famous treaty. How did the haughty queen react to the sight of her stalwart Champion and bridegroom drooling all over her expensive carpets?" The warrior asked bitterly.

"Lord!" The other man remonstrated. "She is not haughty...well not as bad as some of the city women, and she has just cause. After all, she is the queen."

"Right, I forgot. She's the crystal witch, absolute ruler of the mightiest city on our world, while I'm a lowly desert magician. Rats, I believe they call us in this place."

"Yes, but she won't be ruler of this city until you win it for her, and then she won't be absolute ruler, for you'll share that duty with her. It has been written in the treaty. The elders added it, for they too have doubts that she could be trusted without your influence."

"How clever of my elders, and how stupid of the queen. Come now, nowhere have I heard that she was a fool, so how did they get her to sign that particular document?"

"Well, actually, she didn't have any choice, not once she had made you Champion. Asan went to Shen and the elders of Crystia and demanded that the rights of Champion be spelt out so that later there would be no question of what you could do. A new treaty was written with everything out plain, and since the queen gave Shen the power to act for her in every instance, he was the one who signed the new treaty. After all, he was no warrior and knew nothing of warfare, so he handed over the power to those who were wiser, in this instance, than he was."

The golden warrior shook his head and frowned. "It'll be interesting to see how she responds to that. However, the elders might have been wiser to leave such negotiations until she returned. Oh well, it is done. We will handle that problem when she is safe in her palace." The Ah'Jarl smiled grimly. "Come, my friend, let us go down to the council chambers and see if they have any word of where our queen is."

Still smiling, the tall man led the way down from the tower and into the suite of rooms that had been given to him. The Ah'Jarl still didn't realize the extent of the changes made in the treaty Shen had signed, nor did he realize what the desert elders had done to force Crystal City to accept the additions to the treaty.

The House Lords and the Nomad Elders waited for him in the council room. The elders had been in contact with All'ya, and were busy trying to figure out some way to get the two women into the city. After sitting quietly and listening to them debate the merits of plans ranging from sheer folly to the utter ridiculous, the Ah'Jarl finally interrupted.

"Don't our women go out of the city each day to wash at the river? Have they ever been stopped?"

"Aye Lord, they go in and out. They're stopped and searched each time, so they can't smuggle in anything but information."

"Well then, send out a group and let two of them change places with the queen and All'ya. The two who change places can wait for their men back at their villages. Surely, even a city witch should have learned enough in six months to deceive the guards. She must have some idea of how to act like one of our women unless she is a complete fool."

The House Lords cringed. One of the Desert Chiefs shook his head. "No Lord, be not thinking the queen is a fool, or we'll all be the worse for it. She's a clever and determined woman. Make no error about that."

"All right then, that's what we'll do. Instruct the women and send them out in the morning." The warrior grinned, "Old man, if she's as clever and determined as you claim, how will she react to that new treaty you shoved down her man's throat?" He sensed the House Lords' discomfort at his mention of the new treaty, and briefly wondered if the problems he'd been having with them was because they resented the terms of the treaty. 'Quarl rejected that thought. If they didn't like the wording of the treaty, then they should not have signed it.

The old man shook his head. "Well, we're hoping that she'll see the reason behind it."

"Sure, before or after she chops your head off?" the warrior asked sardonically.

As he started to leave the room, Shen walked in, "Alex has her." He said briefly.

'Quarl frowned at the obvious relief on the House Lords' faces. "Alex who?" He asked sharply.

"Our most beloved and wise cousin," Shen explained with a grin as the House Leaders all chuckled.

"How do you know that he has her? Is he wizard trained?"

"Solari, a Named Crystal Guardian and Alex's mate, told me." Shen answered shortly.

*****

Alex opened his eyes just as the sun set, stared at the horizon for a moment, then relaxed. "We wait until full dark." He whispered.

"Someone comes." All'ya whispered, a few hours later.

Alex smiled, "Yes, I rather expected him."

"Who is it?" Mar'ya asked.

"Lie still and listen. He has been coming to this spot every night for a week."

The medium-sized shadow stopped about three feet from where they lay, turned and faced the tall peak of Mist Mountain. He bowed and stood silent for a minute.

"Crystal, tell me what to do." The voice of an old man that sounded vaguely familiar, whispered into the night. "They took my girl. The wizards said they were training her. They said that she would be a greater witch than even the queen. I was so proud, so happy for her. I never questioned, never doubted; I let them take my beautiful Trina."

The old man paused. When he continued, his voice was hoarse with unshed tears. "Crystal, they took my child, and when they returned, they told me to bring my warriors here, that my Trina was waiting for me. I let myself be tricked: I let my pride turn my face from what I knew was right and followed the wizards to find my daughter. My Trina, she was a plaything for the wizards. They laughed at me, said she had been well trained to do the only thing women were fit to do. Now they want me to help them. They hold my daughter. She will do anything they tell her, and when she looks at me, there is hatred in her eyes. The wizards have taken her mind, and she will obey them.

"I drug my child. Each night I bring her here. Crystal, guide me, House Slee is only a small mining House. We are not great and powerful, and my warriors are unhappy. They know I have led them astray. They want to go home, but I cannot leave my child, my daughter who hates me, nor can I take her with me, for her mind would lead the wizards and the larger Houses to me and my people would perish." With those words, the old man fell to his knees and began to cry.

Before anyone could stop her, Mar'ya crawled behind the sobbing man, and put her arms around him, "Hush, Malik, for I will take your daughter and remove the poison from her mind and her heart. I will hold her safe. Take your warriors and guard the mountains of Frya. Let none but the faithful pass. That is your reward, but this is your punishment: House Slee is no more. Its mines, its wealth, and its homes will be given into the care of House Frya. From now until the end of time, you are an old man of House Frya, and your warriors are of House Frya. Your allegiance is now to Shen, House Frya. Go and serve your new lord faithfully."

The old man did not turn, but he raised his arm and two warriors, carrying a bundle between them, came into view. They lay the bundle in the grass, then left. Malik stood, turned north and walked away, followed by the shadows of his warriors.

All'ya crawled up to where a weeping Mar'ya still knelt, "You are a fool." She whispered gently.

Mar'ya ignored that statement, "All'ya, leave me to Alex. He will get me safely to the city. Take our damaged sister to the desert and beg them to keep her safe for me."

"Mar'ya, I will not beg. I will not need to." All'ya turned to Alex, "Help me get her to the riding beasts. Mar'ya, your love for your people has proven that you are indeed worthy to be queen of the desert. You have honored me with your friendship. My life is forever yours." All'ya whispered, then she was gone.

When Alex returned, Mar'ya was still kneeling in the grass, staring to the southwest, watching the flickering campfires of her enemies.

He touched her shoulder and whispered, "Let's go. The most dangerous part of your trip is still ahead of you. I hope the nomads trained you to move with the wind."

For the next two nights, Alex and Mar'ya traveled north toward the foothills of the Great

Mountain range. During the day, they hid among the rocks and low bushes that dotted the landscape. Mar'ya wept every time a patrol wearing the colors of a Crystal House passed by. A grim-faced Alex watched her quietly.

"Cousin, we are almost safe. Tonight you will be beyond the searchers, and by tomorrow morning, you will be safely in the castle."

"Do you think I weep because of the hardships, Alex?" Mar'ya could not hide the bitterness in her voice.

"I know why you weep, Cousin. You weep for your people, you weep with the pain of betrayal; you weep because the damn Crystal is weeping. She does you no favor, holding you so close. I tell you truth, your parents would be proud of you." Alex explained as he led her down a small, dark tunnel.

"My mother, yes. My father," Mar'ya laughed bitterly, "I don't think he would be very proud of my efforts to undo all that he had labored so hard to set into motion."

Alex frowned, "What does Marical Qualdar have to do with this?"

Mar'ya was very still for a moment, then she bent over and became violently ill. "Oh Crystal.

Alex, Richard knew. He knew who my true father was."

"Well, your mother never made any secret of the fact that she loved Marical since she was ten years old. I certainly know that he suspected, but he had no proof." Alex smiled, "Even with proof, he could do nothing."

"He sent Shen to me on my sixteenth birthday," Mar'ya's stomach heaved, as Alex turned to stare at her in shock.

Then he grinned, "So, my little cousin is still a virgin. Shen knew who you were, how did he manage to avoid …." Alex paused.

"Doing his duty?" Mar'ya snarled, "That's how he oh-so-delicately put it as he convinced me that he had no interest in women."

Alex buried his face in the ground, shoulders shaking. He lifted his tear-streaked, dirty face, caught sight of Mar'ya's look of outrage, and collapsed again.

"My family finds me so amusing?" Mar'ya's voice was silky smooth.

"No, no, its just Shen, not interested in women? Oh Crystal," Alex glanced at Mar'ya, "Why are you looking so put out? Did you want him?"

"Alex! That's disgusting! No, I did not want him, it's just…" Mar'ya paused trying to sort out why she was so disgruntled. "It's a woman thing. You would not understand." She said loft-ily, which set Alex off again.

"Did everyone in the castle know but me?"

"Well I knew, but then, I know everything."

"You didn't know who Richard sent to my room."

"No. I never tried to find out."

"Why not?"

"Because, Sweet Cousin, I would have killed him."

"Oh."

They traveled in silence for a while, then Mar'ya sat on the path, her legs stretched out before her.

"Are you tired?" Alex sat next to her.

"No, it's just… I am surprised by how much you care for me."

"I know. It really is quite astonishing how many people love you when you are such a terrible, spoiled, little brat."

"More people hate me."

"Mar'ya, not all of our people hate you. Most of the house warriors don't know you.

They swear fealty to their House Lords. Look at the people in the city. Not one House based in the city betrayed you, and even the ordinary people in the city know and love you."

"Hmm, so Shen really does like women?"

Alex grinned, "He has a certain reputation in that area, yes. What are you planning?"

Mar'ya grinned, "I'll let you know."

"I am your most humble slave. If I can help in any way, do not hesitate to call."

"Pig."

"You wound me, Majesty." Alex lay back, his arms under his head.

"How did you and Solari meet?" Mar'ya stared at her dirty hands.

"I walked out of the northern desert and there she was, on the same road heading towards the Mountains of Frya. One look at her and I fell on my knees and asked her to marry me."

"What did she say?"

Alex chuckled, "She pushed me down with her feet, and told me to come see her when I had taken a bath. Two years later, we were married."

"It took you two years to take a bath?" Mar'ya laughed.

"Brat." Alex pulled her hair.

"Alex, what were you doing in the desert?"

"Growing up. My father was your mother's uncle, but he married a nomad woman. I had an older brother. He had one son. Solari and I have no children."

Mar'ya sat up, "You were raised in the desert?"

Alex nodded, "Yep."

"How did you become the family spy?"

"You are the first person to ask me about my past. Everyone else just took for granted that I was raised in one of the other Houses." Alex stood and stretched, "Don't you want to know who my nephew is? *You* have met him before."

Mar'ya stared at him. Suspicion flared in her dark brown eyes, "No, I don't want to know," she said and stood up, brushing her hands on her clothes.

Alex laughed, "Sure?"

"Certain." Mar'ya said firmly.

Chapter Sixteen

Ten hours later, two dirty, tired figures stumbled into the castle's basement, and climbed the long flight of stairs up to the dining hall. The sound of the door opening caused Shen to glance up from his plate.

"Mar'ya!" He knocked over his chair, as he rushed to her side, closely followed by Pat and Carol, "Oh, thank Crystal you are all right."

Mar'ya smiled happily, "I'm starving and tired," she walked to the table and snagged a breakfast roll, "And so very happy to be home," she mumbled around a mouthful of bread.

In a dark corner of the room, 'Quarl studied the woman who had so disrupted his life.

"Mar'ya," Pat reached to take the rest of the bread from Mar'ya's hand. "Your hands are dirty."

Mar'ya avoided Pat and stuffed the last of the bread into her mouth, then glanced down at her hands and shrugged happily.

"Tea?" she choked.

Carol laughed and poured a cup of tea, while Pat took charge. "Okay, you are home. It took Alex three days to get you here." She winked at Alex, "We are very happy to see you; at least we think it's you under all the dirt. What did you do? Dig into the castle with your hands?"

Mar'ya took the cup from Carol and drank a big swallow of hot tea before she answered. "Something like that, but Alex kept using his face." She giggled.

"Alex, go home. Clean up and let Solari treat your wounds," Pat ordered.

"They are not wounds," Alex objected, "Just a few scratches, and bruises."

Pat pointed to the door, "Go!"

Alex went. Pat turned to her swaying queen. "You are going to your rooms, young lady. Bath and bed."

"No. I have to find out how things are going; see 'Ulan, visit with the Ah'Jarl. I have too much to do to rest right now." Mar'ya's voice trailed off as she collapsed unconscious into Pat's motherly arms.

Pat carried the queen out of the room with Shen trailing worriedly behind them. 'Quarl stepped out of his corner, a frown on his face. The happy, giggling woman-child he just watched instilled no confidence, yet Asan feared her as if she were a demon. 'Ulan held her in the highest esteem, most of his warriors respected her, and her people worshipped her. She was a total contradiction, and nothing like he expected.

'Quarl had just poured himself a fresh cup of tea, when 'Ulan ran into the room, "Ah'Jarl, did you see All'ya?"

'Quarl shook his head, "No, but I think the crystal witch wanted to speak with you." 'Quarl realized he was speaking to an empty room as 'Ulan headed up the stairs.

Shen stood outside the queen's chambers, staring at the closed door with a bemused expression. "Shen, where is All'ya?" 'Ulan demanded.

"She went back to the desert for some reason, but I was to tell you your betrothed is alive and very well. Alex gave me the message. He had to sneak back in to tell me."

"The queen, how is she?" 'Ulan glanced at the closed door.

Shen shook his head, "She is dirty and tired and the women will take care of her; that's all they told me before I was thrown out of the room."

"It is good that she is back." 'Ulan leaned against the wall next to Shen.

"It is indeed, my friend, it is indeed." Shen smiled at his new friend.

*****

"Commander Charles, do you want our platoon to fill the open spot in the northeast?"

Charles glanced at the young trooper before him, and frowned. "That is Slue, Slaw…"

"Slee, sir." The young man interrupted.

Charles waved a hand, "Whoever. These barbarians and their outlandish names, I never can remember them. Anyway, isn't Slee supposed to be covering that area?"

"Sir, we have not seen any member of House Slee in three days. We think some of the other Houses have been covering for them."

Charles snorted, "Once a traitor, always a traitor. Let me speak to the emperor and see what he wants you to do. In the meantime, stay put."

"Sir, yes sir." The young man saluted and walked off. Charles watched him then stood and went to see his emperor.

"No. I do not want any of my people close to that city," Gregor snarled.

"My Emperor…" Charles began.

"This war is going to be a thing for the wizards, and I do not want any of you in harm's way." Gregor winced, and rubbed his head.

Bells rang out and Crystal City glowed brightly for a moment, then darkness and silence returned to the plains.

Gregor looked at Charles and sighed, "So it begins," he whispered.

*****

The wizards met in their own tent later that night. "How could she have entered the city without our knowledge? Did Barak teach her how to block her mind from us?" Bunji scowled

"Would she have the power to take it from his mind without his being aware?"

Rede shook his head. "No, Master Bunji, there is no way she learned that skill from him," Rede smiled, "Barak did not have that particular skill. In truth, he was the most inept wizard I have ever met. That is, after all, why he was chosen to train the crystal witch. If it is true that she has been in the mountains, then Crystal herself could have shielded her from us."

"That would mean Crystal knows what we have been up to." One of the younger wizards protested.

"The Crystal Bitch knows. She has been aware of our aims since we first landed on this continent." Bunji turned his attention back to Rede. "Rede, why don't you think that the young queen may have spent her time on her holy mountain?"

Rede sighed, "I know you don't want to hear this, but I suspect that she may have been in one of the holy places of the desert people. I think we are making a big mistake in dismissing their magic as unimportant. Remember, they are Stone's people. There is a strong force among them, and I fear it will tilt this battle against us."

The other wizards laughed, and Bunji frowned. "Rede, you've been away from us too long. The nomads are savages. Stone has been chained for centuries, and he was always a weakling and a fool. I'll hear no more about the desert folk magic. We will assume that Crystal is at last coming out of hiding. She is showing her strength by helping her chosen to get into the castle undetected. Fine. This time, she caught us unprepared; the next time we will be ready for her."

*****

Early the next morning, the city's bells rang. When the people answered the call, they saw their queen, her dark hair blowing wildly in the breeze, standing on the castle's second floor balcony. Mar'ya waved happily, and her people waved back.

'Quarl stood next to some of his warriors on the ground and watched the show. "Are they happy to see her?" He asked the warrior next to him.

"Look at their faces." The warrior advised. "They are glowing. There won't be any cheers. It's not the time for that, but yes, I would say they are very happy to see her."

'Quarl watched a few more seconds, then turned and went back into the castle. As he walked toward the council chamber, the sound of bells from the left caught his attention. The air shimmered, and three people appeared in the hallway. He recognized two of them: His mother, Vera, Speaker for Stone and All'ya. The third woman was a stranger, but her dark hair marked her as a child of Crystal. Before he could greet them, the door to the castle's chapel opened and the Crystal Guardians stepped out and approached the newcomers. 'Quarl sighed and continued to the council chamber.

A few minutes later, All'ya and 'Ulan joined him, followed by the rest of the council members. Shen and the Crystal Guardians walked in last and stood in a semi-circle behind the crystal throne.

*****

The young queen smiled happily as she entered her room. "Mase, the people look good. I wonder why the empire has not attacked us yet?"

Mase shrugged, "Last I heard, they were trying to talk the Crystal Guardians into naming their emperor, lord of our city, then they started all sorts of nasty rumors that you were dead and that the nomads were responsible."

Mar'ya stood before the mirror as she fussed and fretted with the fit of her dress until Mase threw her hands in the air, "Child, you may be a grown woman and my queen, but if you don't settle down right now, I'll spank you."

"Oh Mase, I'm sorry, but I just don't feel comfortable in these clothes anymore. They restrict my movements, and there are too many ruffles."

"Fine, no ruffles." The old woman tore the offending frills off the dress. "That's the best I can do. You're a queen. You must look the part. No one ever said you had to be comfortable at the same time. Are you ready to go down and meet what is left of your council, and also that great hulk you have named Champion?"

"Oh, he's better then? I'm so pleased. What's he like?" the queen asked eagerly.

"Well, he's a man. Just like the rest of his kind, I suppose. Though cleaner than the rest of them. He shaves his face, but that's no improvement. I think he'd look better if he let his beard grow. He's a great, ugly man. I shudder to think of you with him. Can't you find another way to keep your throne?"

"No. I have made my choices, and now I must live with them." The queen hugged the other woman and walked down the stairs to her council room.

The remaining House Lords, the Desert Elders, 'Ulan, All'ya, Shen and the Crystal Guardians were all in the room. There was a somberness to the gathering that caused Mar'ya to shiver. Something was wrong. She glanced around the room and saw, standing in a dark corner, one she knew was her Champion. He was wearing a sardonic smile on his scarred face and there was a mocking look in his eyes. *So, my Champion knows what is wrong and he is watching to see how I am going to react.*

She smiled at him. In response, he lifted one heavy brow, but did not smile back. *All right, two can play this game.* Mar'ya decided, *I do not know what is wrong, but I vow that I will not lose my temper in the council chambers. I am an adult now, and I will act accordingly.* With a slight shrug, she turned away, *I will deal with my Champion later. He really isn't all that ugly, though he is not as handsome as his uncle.* A small smile tugged at the corner of her mouth as she mounted the dais and took her place at the head of the table.

"Doth my Champion wish to sit in on this meeting, or is he content to sulk in the shadows?" she asked with false sweetness.

The man bowed slightly to her. A glimmer of a smile touched his eyes but was gone so quickly she doubted it had been there. He walked with long, confident strides, to the table and sat with his people.

She sighed. "My Lord, you're here as my Champion tonight, therefore you should sit by me. It's demanded by custom and by courtesy, no matter what our inclination in the matter."

Her lips tightened when she saw he had no intentions of moving. *I will not become angry over this insult because something in the way everyone is watching me says that before the night is over, I will have just cause to lose my temper.*

"Your Highness." Shen stood up slowly, "I would give report on my stewardship." He looked at her hesitantly.

So, Shen has done something that I am not going to like. Shen? she wondered in amusement, *my cousin, my brother, who has protected me for so many years. There is something amiss...*

"So Shen, what have the desert folk talked you into doing now?" She smiled. It quickly disappeared when she saw the reactions of those around her.

"Shen, I would hear thee." Her voice was quiet and metal cold.

"Lady, 'Ulan and the Northern Desert Tribe have walked in honor." Shen said quickly.

Mar'ya nodded, "I expected no less. 'Ulan, we honor you and yours." She raised an eyebrow, "What else do you need to tell me?"

"Your Highness, read." Shen pushed the papers at her and sat down quickly, his face pale.

The rest of her people pushed their chairs back from the table and looked as if they expected to bolt at any second.

The Warrior Mage was surprised. These people were genuinely afraid of the calm, young woman at the head of the table. He frowned and tensed his body. His nostrils flared as he tried to scent out danger for his people.

Mar'ya read the paper quickly, then frowned and reread it as if she did not believe what her first reading told her. She very calmly set the papers down on the table in front of her, and stared at her hands for a moment.

"Shen, why did you sign this? Did you even read it first?"

"Your Highness, the Elder, Asan, said that he would take the nomad tribes and leave the city. 'Ulan, refused to take his men away, and was insulted by Asan. I signed, Your Highness, because 'Ulan assured me that you were alive and well. I trusted you to handle this situation."

Mar'ya handed the papers to Vera, then turned back to the table. "I see. You did not trust me. That is your right. You used coercion on my people to force the signing of this paper. That is not your right. I would have agreed to most of this. Most of these terms are implicit in the word 'Champion'. There would have been no conflict. I trusted you." She turned again to Vera, "You said, 'Let there be honor between yours and mine, and between mine and yours.' If this is your concept of honor, then I pity you and your people."

"Hold, Daughter of Crystal," Vera stepped forward, "Do not dishonor all my people because of the actions of one."

"I hold 'Ulan, his people, and All'ya, swordswoman, in great honor, but how many others of your people objected to Asan's behavior?" Mar'ya stared at the shamed faces of the Nomad Elders and nodded grimly.

"I trusted your honor and this is my repayment. I do not approve of your methods. Hear me. I consider you all forsworn and without honor. I will deal with you after we have settled the western empire and its wizards. Again, hear me." Her voice sounded like the whisper of a sword being drawn. A gasp went around the table. Asan jumped to his feet.

"Sit down, Asan." Vera snapped, "You have caused enough problems."

"None may call my people forsworn." 'Quarl leaned on the table toward the young queen, his voice just as deadly as hers had been.

She nodded at him. "Fine. First you'll serve as my Champion. Afterward, you will Champion your people."

"Who will be your Champion?"

"I need no champion to protect me from those who are forsworn. I'll be my own champion. I've given my word: You are my Champion, that won't change. But the condition under which we live, that is your decision. I have spoken. Hear me." She stood, and, with her lips tightly compressed, she left the room.

I will remain in control, I am an adult and the queen of a country in harm's way. I must maintain control. Mar'ya kept that litany going in her head until she reached her rooms. She closed her door quietly. Then turned to Mase, "It might be better if you waited outside." She said calmly.

Mase gave her a startled look, and stepped outside the door to stand between the guards.

Asan promised that he would not hold anything he saw in my heart against me. If he found that he could not trust me, then he should have waited until I returned from the desert to confront me. He is a coward, a a a, "Haargh!" Mar'ya's scream echoed through her room, as she swept perfume jars and figurines off her dressing table. In the hallway, the guards and Mase pretended to hear nothing.

*****

The warrior turned to the shaken people left behind in the council room and said very softly, "I think I should read that new treaty. I have not read it before, and it seems that I was remiss in not doing so."

The Speaker handed him the paper, and 'Quarl sat down to read it. He shook his head and looked at his people sadly.

"Do you think I'm a child and not able to take care of myself? Did you have to go to such extremes to protect me?"

He glanced around the table at the shamed faces of his people. "What means did you use to force Shen to sign this humiliating piece of paper? Tell me Shen exaggerated the extent of your threat."

"We did threaten to leave the city unprotected, Ah'Jarl. Asan looked into her heart. He told us that she would betray you, so we followed him," one of the elders finally spoke.

"Are you all children, that you follow even when you know it wrong? I swore that we would aid her. Would you have had me forsworn along with you?" he snarled. "I know not what will come of this piece of mischief, but answer me this: If you trusted her so little, then how could you have sent her to the inner sanctum of our people?"

"We had planned this already, Lord, and thought that it would give safety to both our places and yourself." Asan answered.

"Damn," 'Quarl hissed, and, holding the paper in his hands, left the room.

*****

"Fool, useless old fool." Vera, walked up to Asan and slapped him. "We have waited so long for this time to come, and you in your arrogance would destroy our god's chance to be free. You would destroy the prophecy and our people."

"She would have betrayed us, just as her god betrayed ours. I looked into her heart. She was disgusted by our Ah'Jarl, and looked for ways to deny him."

"The Ah'Jarl is my son and at times, he disgusts me. Look at how he was when she first met him. Under the circumstances, I don't blame her. Did anyone beside 'Ulan give her the benefit of the doubt?"

Asan stared at the Speaker, "The chief of the Northern Desert Tribe was her choice to replace the Ah'Jarl. I feared that he had been corrupted by her, and no longer had the welfare of the desert at heart."

'Ulan tensed, and All'ya snarled, "How dare you, you senile old man. Your life is forfeit. To the swordswomen of the nomads you are dead." She turned her back to Asan.

'Ulan stared at Asan for a long moment, "Elder Asan, to the Northern Desert Tribe, you are dead." He nodded and turned his back as well.

"Asan, go to the desert, and give your life to the Stones." Vera said sadly.

"No! I have done nothing wrong. All that I have done was to protect the Ah'Jarl. Given the choice, I would do the same thing again." Asan protested loudly.

"All'ya, swordswoman, give his life to Stone." Vera turned her back. All'ya spun. Her swords flashed, and Asan's lifeless body collapsed.

Her back still turned, Vera addressed the remaining Elders, "I leave you to the care of the crystal witch, she who will become queen of our people. She may be more merciful than I."

Shen stared at the pool of blood slowly spreading across the council chamber's floor and turned to the guards, "Call housekeeping to clean this up before the queen returns." He sighed, "Housekeeping is getting a lot of experience taking bloodstains off the floor."

Chapter Seventeen

'Quarl strode quickly up to Mar'ya's rooms, only to find his path blocked by a small, frightened, old woman.

"Go away. You have done enough damage, you and them savages of yours. Go on, get out of here. I'll not be telling herself that you're here."

Impatiently, he lifted the old woman aside and walked into the room, stopping in sheer astonishment as he beheld the wreckage before him. Only his warrior's training allowed him to duck his head in time to miss a huge wooden statue the queen threw in his direction.

"Go to your rooms, Mase, I'll deal with this scoundrel myself." Mar'ya snarled as she picked up another statue. With a small squeak, the old woman covered her head and fled. The warrior and the witch stood glaring at each other on opposite sides of the room.

"If you throw that at me, I shall, most assuredly throw it back, and I promise that I won't miss," the Ah'Jarl said quietly.

Mar'ya glanced at the wooden vase in her hands and shrugged. "I never throw things at people." She replied calmly as she set the vase down on her desk and began picking up the other objects that littered the floor.

'Quarl noticed that most of the objects were wood or silver, and not breakable. He picked up a cushion, "May I sit?" He asked.

Mar'ya ignored him as she continued cleaning up the mess. "I didn't expect you to come up here."

"We need to talk." 'Quarl placed the cushion on a chair and sat.

Mar'ya stared around her room and walked to her window. "Why has the empire not attacked us?" She pulled the drapes back and stared out at the city.

'Quarl took a deep breath. "I don't know, shall I go down and asked them?"

Mar'ya, her back to him, smirked, "Yes, please." Her voice was quiet.

The Ah'Jarl stared at her, "Are you serious?"

"Well, you did offer." Mar'ya replied.

'Quarl sighed. This was not going at all how he imagined it would. "Can we start over? I am 'Quarl, the Ah'Jarl of the desert, your Champion."

"I know who you are; you are 'Quarl, the Ah'Jarl, who has humiliated me, ignored me, and whose people betrayed me. I will not say 'pleased to meet you'. However, I am pleased that you have recovered." Mar'ya's voice was cold.

"I have no excuse for what happened, I trusted my people and never thought they would do such a thing. I apologize for my people's actions."

"Did you talk to Shen? Did you ask 'Ulan what was going on? The only person you spoke to was Asan. Every word he said, you took as truth. Not once did you question my people as to what was going on." Mar'ya stopped and took a deep breath.

"Calm down. I admitted I was wrong. What more do you want?" 'Quarl interrupted.

"Calm down? I was calm in the council hall, but these are my rooms, and I can act any way I please in here. As for what I want, I want my ability to trust restored. Can you do that? If you are going to talk about that scurrilous piece of paper, then you can take your great, ugly face and march right out of here. Your people are misnamed, they're not rats, they're snakes. They couldn't wait to get me out of the palace so they could slither behind my back and announce to the whole world that my word as a ruler is not to be trusted."

Grimly, the warrior walked across the room and stood next to Mar'ya. "Now listen to me, Queen of Crystia, I had not read this paper before. As a matter of fact, I knew little of it, but my people thought they were protecting me. They find it hard to trust a city witch. Now, let us try to find some way to work past this. I have apologized to you, I will apologize to your council and the Crystal Guardians if you wish.

For now, however, let me show you what I think of this paper."

He walked over to the fire, tore the document in half, and threw the pieces into the flames. He turned to her. "Now, it's done. It never has been. Do you understand? It's finished."

Mar'ya glanced up at him angrily, "Your people are still forsworn. I trusted them. Whatever they thought was in my heart, could they not have trusted me as the Holder of the Crystal Throne to keep my word? I trusted them despite the advice of my council, and they have betrayed that trust."

The man bowed his head, then he looked at her sadly, "My people are forsworn, and the debt is mine. Shall I pay now?"

Mar'ya took a deep breath and reined in her temper. "No." She reached out her hand then dropped it to her side without touching him. "Your death will avail nothing. It would defeat me, and give the Crystal Throne to the western emperor. You must live. After this is over, we will talk again of what penance I will demand from your people."

"I'm still your Champion then?"

"And still my Chosen. I'm called Mar'ya, 'she who passed through darkness to bring light'."

He nodded, thinking it a fitting name for her. "I am 'Quarl, the Ah'Jarl, 'he who protects'. This one is proud to be Champion of the crystal witch."

"So, mighty protector, tell me: What else has been happening while I was gone."

"Not much, the empire laid siege to the city, then Gregor started applying to the Guardians to name him heir to the Crystal Throne. They tried to convince the people that you were dead and that my people were to blame. That did not work. Now, I have no idea what they are waiting for, or what is going on."

"I might have an idea. The wizards are enemies of both Crystal and Stone, but we have all forgotten there were four gods in the beginning…"

"Mist." 'Quarl shook his head, "Mist has no dealing with humans."

"I don't know what else it could be." Mar'ya frowned.

"How about they are trying to starve us out? That way, they get the city undamaged, with no loss of life to their people."

"Then it's up to us to do something before our people begin to suffer. Damn. Do all my cousins have nothing better to do than give me bad news?"

'Quarl looked at her startled, "So you know."

"I know everything." Mar'ya stuck her little nose in the air.

'Quarl threw back his head and laughed aloud. "Oh really."

"Yes, really." Mar'ya studied 'Quarl's face and sighed. "It's a shame you're not as handsome as your uncle. How did you get that scar?"

'Quarl's voice was tightly controlled when he answered, "I fell when I was a child and cut my face on a stone."

Mar'ya laughed, "Oh. Here I thought it was something heroic, a sword cut from a duel of honor, or a jealous husband." Her laughter died as she glanced at him and caught the old pain deep in his eyes. "It must have hurt a lot." She said quietly.

'Quarl stared out the window, "Yeah, I was only six at the time. My mother, Alex and I were on our way home when it happened. We had been to visit Solari, and I was jumping from rock to rock, not really paying attention, when I slipped. I hit my head pretty hard, I was unconscious for days. They thought I would lose my eye so no one worried much about something as minor as a little scar." There was a hint of bitterness in his voice.

Mar'ya giggled, "Oh your poor head, you always seem to hurt it. I hope it isn't the softest part of your body."

'Quarl gave a startled look, "Have we met before?"

"I don't think so. Why?"

"I've heard you laugh before."

"Well it must have been a long time ago, I haven't laughed in years."

'Quarl frowned, "It was a long time, before I fell." He said slowly.

Mar'ya closed her eyes trying to remember, "Can you cross your eyes?"

They stared at each other then smiled at the memory that drifted between them.

"You could grow a beard," Mar'ya finally offered shyly, picking up the previous conversation.

"No." 'Quarl's reply was short.

"Why?" Mar'ya was curious.

"Do your men have beards?" He asked.

"No, my people don't have facial hair. Oh." Mar'ya grinned. She couldn't help herself, it was funny. She turned and stared at him, "Scraggly huh?"

"Do you always make such blunt statements? You could hurt someone's feelings you know."

Mar'ya blushed, "I'm always being told to think before I speak, but sometimes I forget. That's one of my worst failings, I speak heedlessly at times. I also have a rotten temper." She smiled shyly, "Well, I thought that you should know the worst about me right at the beginning."

"That's all right, I can live with those faults. I'm not perfect either." He smiled at her look of pretend surprise. "Is there anything else about you I should know before we go any further with this relationship?" He asked, and then watched in amazement as the color ran up her face.

"Ahh, so there is something. What is it?"

"Nothing." Mar'ya walked away from him, "I think you should leave now. Anything else that is necessary, you'll find out in time."

She gave him a very false, but brilliant smile and fled the sitting room, slamming her bedroom door behind her.

'Quarl sat in stunned surprise, *Well, that was surprising. I wonder what she is hiding. I am going to have a long talk with All'ya and find out exactly what she discovered about our young queen. First, though, we have to do something about the army outside the walls.*

Knocking softly on her door, he called, "Mar'ya, come on out. We have to discuss how to rid ourselves of the wizards and their puppet.

From behind the door Mar'ya questioned, "You think Gregor is only a tool of the Wizard Council? I thought it was the other way around."

"Take my word for it, Mar'ya, his heart is not in this fight. If we can eliminate the wizards, Emperor Gregor will be no problem. I suggest you stop sulking and join me in the council chambers. We have a lot of planning to do. We can iron out our differences later. Right now, we need a plan to eliminate the army around the city. Come. The chiefs of both our people are waiting for us."

Mar'ya closed her eyes. She was not ready to face anyone just yet, but the Ah'Jarl was right. They had to eliminate the empire from the scene, that should be her only worry now. The future would take care of itself. With that thought, Mar'ya gathered her composure and left her room. Together, the witch and the warrior walked down the long halls toward the council chamber as if nothing ever happened between them.

The large, sun-lit room was silent when the witch and the warrior entered. There was a shamed quality to the silence.

Mar'ya's lips tightened, "I know you are expecting me to throw a tantrum. Well, I'm not going to. I am your queen and my country is in jeopardy. It's time I grew up. However, I am not going to say anything soothing or reassuring. I don't want to. What I want to do is find a dark place to weep until my disappointment in those I trusted has been washed away. That, however, would not be productive.

"There is an enemy outside the gates of this city that would destroy all we hold dear in Stoneland Desert and Crystia. Let us not make it any easier than we already have for them."

Mar'ya sighed as she took her place at the head of the long table and counted the empty spaces. "Thirteen of these great, carved chairs are empty. Those who occupied them have betrayed all we hold dear. It is up to those of us who remain to make them regret that betrayal."

As Mar'ya waited for 'Quarl and the others to sit, she silently named the Houses left: Frya from the North; Capra from the South; Sa from the West; Orin and Tau from the East, Sua from the central plains. Two of the Warrior Houses remained: Mar, and Kel. The only group that had no traitor Houses were the Merchant Houses: Agon, Trata, Paron, and House Sultav of the Shadows.

The majority of the Large Houses had turned traitor. She had to hold the remainder of her people together. Mar'ya waited another long heartbeat before she broke the silence. "I understand you thought you were protecting your

Lord," she said to the desert elders. "Mayhap you saw in my heart that which made it difficult to trust me. So be it, for now." She turned to her own people. "You did what was needful to protect our city. On you, there is no blame." She smiled around the room, "So, let us get down to planning how to rid ourselves of the western empire its emperor, the traitors among our own people, and the Wizard Council."

"Lady, may I speak? I am Rowan, cousin to Gail, Mistress of House Frya and Guardian of the Holy Mountains. I am second in the Council of the Named Crystal Guardians. Last night, Crystal herself spoke to the Guardians; I have been sent to give this council her words." The woman paused.

"Speak, Guardian Rowan. What message has the Lady given to the Guardians?"

"Thus spoke the Lady Crystal: 'To defeat the enemy without, first you must defeat the enemy within. Fire and ice must become one, and remain unchanged. The maid must become mother, and the warrior must become priest. Find the stones that speak and the water that falls in the heart of the desert, then discover the fires that can not be quenched.

"'When this is done, come to me, bring proof to the Crystal that Burns that you have met my conditions. This must be done before the third day. Then, at the height of the sun, I, the Goddess known as Crystal, will move the very earth, and change the world as you know it. I will give to my witch and her Champion the power to destroy their enemies, and bring the Wizard Council to their knees.

"'Listen well, Daughter: Call in the faithful. Cause them to abandon the beaches. Secure House Frya in the high mountains. Tread with care on the Forest paths. For I shall cause the desert to bloom, and the trees to fall. The mountain will move, and the sea shall claim much of the land.'

"The Guardians have sent out the warning to the faithful Houses. House Frya has been secured; the remnants of House Slee, which is no more, have been taken into the safe places of the mountain. The desert folk have aided the people of loyal Houses that still remain outside the city. All that remains is for you to solve the riddle, then Crystal will walk once more among her people, and the division between our people and the desert dwellers will be healed."

Mar'ya stared at the Crystal Guardians, then sighed, "Oh great. Riddles. And only three days to solve them in. I hate riddles." Mar'ya bent her head and closed her eyes. "All right people, let's get on it. If I'm the maid that is to become mother, then I don't think three days is long enough for that." She blushed when she noticed the surprised looks that flashed around the room. Obviously, her secret was no longer. It was not important. Nothing was, except for the solution to Crystal's riddles.

"No, I have to agree with you on that," the Warrior grinned. So that was why the queen was upset earlier. "Unfortunately, it would take at least nine months. Anyway, the goddess would never give us anything so straightforward. The gods don't work that way. I don't think that's quite what she meant. Let us start with the things we know. The stones that speak, and the water that rushes in the heart of the desert: These things are a part of the landscape. How do we bring them to Crystal in three days?"

"Well, we couldn't do that, even if we could do the rest of it, since the Crystal that Burns is in the heart of Crystal Mountain at least a week of hard travel from here. There is no way to get there by magic, so now what?"

Vera, the Speaker for Stone, spoke up then, "It must be all symbols. The maid must become symbolically mother. You have done that. You have put aside your own anger and pain to do that which is best for your people, and thus behaved as a mother to them. Warrior, when you healed the damage done to your mind you acted as a priest, for only the priests have the power to heal broken minds."

Mar'ya glanced at the thoughtful faces around the room. "Yes, all right, I'll accept that. So what do the rest of the symbols mean? What or who is the enemy within? I hope no one else is planning to betray me. I don't think I could stand anymore of that." Mar'ya frowned, though her words were spoken lightly. "What is this fire and ice that must become one without changing? There is no way that could be."

"My Lady," Rowan spoke, "The fire is Stoneland, and the ice is Crystia. There are two possible interpretations, the first is the treaty that we of the city have signed; the second, is the formal joining of the Desert Mage and the Crystal Witch. With both of these, we have a joining of fire and ice, without any changes in the basic character of either."

The warrior nodded, "You could be right, Crystal Guardian. What do we know so far? If we take the riddle to be speaking of symbols, and not the actual thing, then the queen and I have already met two of the conditions. She has become a true mother to her people, and I have become a true priest among my people.

"Next, we will have to go through the ceremony to become life mates before the gods of both our people..."

"That's it," Mar'ya interrupted. "The ceremony: Our taking the life vows is to be held before a piece of the Crystal that Burns here in the castle's temple. So that's where we're to take the symbols."

"And the witness to that ceremony will be those who represent the other things. Vera, the Speaker of the desert tribes, would represent the stones that speak, but who would represent the rushing water thing?" the warrior asked puzzled.

"That one is easy, it would have to be All'ya, the swordswoman who traveled with me." Mar'ya frowned, "That makes no sense. There are no witnesses from among my people, and who or what is the enemy within?" She glanced around the room. "Is one of you a traitor? *I don't think I can stand any more betrayals. In the last six months, I have been betrayed by almost everyone I trusted. Shen and Alex are the only two who have stood by me. I have no confidence in my ability to read the hearts and minds of those around me. If there was another traitor in my midst, I don't think I could survive.*

'Ulan interrupted her thoughts, "Lady, Lord, you must take your life vows, and consummate that mating on the third day at noon, in the Crystal Temple. The witnesses must be All'ya, the swordswoman, and Vera, the Speaker. The fires that cannot be quenched must be the passion that will grow between the two of you. The enemy within is the doubts and fears that each of you holds deep within your own heart. We don't have much time for the two of you to discover what they are and to acknowledge them. They must be seen in the clear light of day and dealt with."

"We are missing something here. The Crystal Goddess would not have me swear to your Ah'Jarl without witnesses from among her faithful. I will grant that you may be right about the enemies within." She paused, "Suppose there is no passionate fire burning between the warrior and myself. Then what do we do?"

"Then we go forth into battle with warrior magic alone. I must warn you, without the magic of the Crystal, we have no hope of defeating the Wizard Council," Vera answered.

Mar'ya slanted a glance at the mage warrior sitting impassively at the other side of the table. While she no longer found him ugly, he stirred no flames in her body. She sighed. *Why do the gods order so much from their followers? I really do not want this man in my bed. He is too large...too...too everything.*

The Crystal Guardians seemed to read Mar'ya's thoughts, "Your Highness, you are no longer a child and this is demanded of you by the gods, and your people."

"I don't think one can create passion at will, Guardian Rowan."

"If the seeds were not present, the goddess would not have demanded it."

"As you will, Guardian." She turned to 'Quarl, "I hope you are better at this passion business than I am," She hissed softly at him.

He grinned wolfishly at her. "Oh, I think I can rise to the occasion."

Mar'ya ignored the snickers around the room and stared at him. She was glad he found the situation amusing. It was not his throne at stake here, but hers. By Crystal, she certainly managed to get herself into some interesting situations.

"Mar'ya beware. Of all inner enemies, self doubt is the worst. You have been well trained. You and your Champion have the power to stop any attack the western emperor and his servants can mount. Remember that, and have faith in your Champion and yourself." Shen said, his voice soft with sympathy.

Chapter Eighteen

'Quarl, stood and walked to where Mar'ya was sitting. "Come, we'll go and discuss this more in private," he said to her softly.

Mar'ya gave a nervous laugh. "Do we have to practice?"

Everyone else in the room smiled at her question. The Ah'Jarl shook his head and took her hands. As they left the room, Mar'ya glanced at the puzzled faces of her people. Rowan gave her a sympathetic smile. Her people were amused but wondering what was wrong with their queen, who was acting like a nervous virgin.

She gave Shen an apologetic look as the door closed behind her. He was going to have to bear the brunt of their questions alone. She knew that he would tell the whole truth, for this was not the time for secrets or lies between allies, no matter how harmless they seemed to be.

"I'm not usually so biddable," she said to the warrior walking softly beside her. "I want to warn you of that now. It's just that in this matter, I think you have much more experience than I do. Being no fool, I bow always to superior knowledge."

The warrior looked down at her calmly, then smiled. "Not that much more. By Stone, woman, I've spent most of my life in study and training. When would I have had the time or the energy to gain all the experience you credit me with? Then there is my face. Unlike my uncle, not many females are falling over themselves to mate with me."

"Oh. Are we in trouble?" Mar'ya faked a worried look. She knew that she was only chattering to hide her nervousness. She didn't want to dig too deeply into her psyche. She was afraid of what she might find.

"I've had my moments, I'm not a complete novice," 'Quarl smiled reassuringly at her, letting her know that he realized what her true worry was. "We're resourceful adults, I'm sure we can work something out. But before that, I suggest we spend some time in your temple to study our inner selves. I know that the city troops, with the help of my tribesmen, can handle any moves the emperor might make."

At the door to the temple's meditation chamber, he turned, touched her cheek lightly, and whispered, "Good hunting, Queen of Crystia. All will be well."

"Good hunting to you also, Warrior."

They entered the large room, sealed the door behind them, and separated, each going to a different corner.

With a small sigh, Mar'ya looked distastefully at the brightly-colored silk cushions on the temple floor. Her tastes had changed drastically during her stay in the desert, and she no longer found this room pleasing. The cushions were too soft and the colors too bright for her to find them soothing. With a snort of disgust, she forced herself to sit. There was nothing wrong with either the room or the cushions.

She was making excuses to avoid looking too closely at her herself. She was not at all eager to begin. Mar'ya stared blindly at the multi-faceted crystal walls covered with bright murals depicting the history of Crystia. She did not see the rainbow of sunlight that reflected into the room and made the pictures dance with life. Mar'ya realized that, deep down, she did not believe she was truly worthy of being the queen her people deserved.

"Champion?"

"Yes Mar'ya." She heard a rustle as 'Quarl began to move.

"No. Stay where you are. It's easier to talk to someone when you can't see them. Are you listening?"

"Yes."

"Is there something wrong with me?"

"I don't think so. Why do you ask?"

"I just wondered if there was something inside me that makes those I trust betray me. I know you destroyed that shameful treaty, but..." Mar'ya paused, "I'm not saying this very well am I?"

"It was not for show. I meant it. I would never betray you, but you must trust me."

"Shen doesn't like you, yet he told me to have faith in you."

"There is a great deal of wisdom in Shen. I wish that I had listened to him earlier. A lot of our problems might have been avoided."

"Shen is not very brave, but he is my brother and my best friend. I will try to do what he said."

There was a long moment of silence, "Mar'ya, is there anything else you want to discuss?"

"No, that's it. Thank you 'Quarl, I think I am ready to begin now."

"Umm, 'Quarl?"

She heard his sigh, "Yes, Mar'ya?"

"Can you still cross your eyes?"

"What?"

"I said…"

"I heard what you said, but is this the time to ask?"

"It's important."

"Yes, Mar'ya, I can still cross my eyes."

"Good, then for a while, will you be six again, before the accident, back in House Frya?"

"I would rather not." 'Quarl's voice was taut.

"Please, this is very important."

"All right, if it will help you settle down."

"Good. Come with me." Mar'ya jumped up and held out her hand to 'Quarl.

"Shh." She placed her fingers over her lips, and moved silently toward the door leading to the inner sanctum of the temple.

"Mar'ya, you are the queen. Why do we have to sneak into the temple?" 'Quarl whispered.

"Because you are six and I'm four and we don't have permission." She whispered back, as she opened the door and peeped into the room. The two of crept to the great crystal in the center of the room, and Mar'ya sat, pulling 'Quarl down with her. Neither of them noticed Alex and Solari sitting against the far wall.

"Crystal," Mar'ya began, "When I was four, I met this wonderful, stinky, little boy. I wanted to introduce him to you because you were so sad, I thought he could cheer you up." She tugged on 'Quarl's arm, "Okay, cross your eyes and stick out your tongue."

"You want me to make a face at your god?" 'Quarl glanced at her in surprise. He could barely make out her vigorous nod in the darkened room. "Are you mad?"

"Just trust me, and do it." There was a stunned silence from both of them as they understood the import of her words.

'Quarl nodded, and very solemnly crossed his eyes and stuck his tongue out at the crystal. The crystal blinked by going dark then glowing again, this behavior continued in time with Mar'ya's giggles. Even 'Quarl chuckled at the obvious glee in both the woman and the crystal.

"I said that I wanted you to be my boyfriend when we grew up." Mar'ya said softly.

'Quarl laughed, "Your standards were not very high back then."

"You made me happy."

"You hurt my feelings. I had just taken a bath that morning."

Mar'ya blinked, "I make it better," she was still four as she threw her arms around his neck, and placed little girl kisses across his face.

'Quarl sat very still, then cleared his throat, "Well, you are about twenty years late, but thanks." He said hoarsely.

Mar'ya blinked, then blushed, "Sorry, I forgot we are all grown up now." She stood and led him back to the meditation chambers, leaving a giggling crystal behind them.

"Are you ready to settle down now, or do you want to put this off even longer?" 'Quarl asked mildly.

"That obvious huh?" Mar'ya stepped behind the privacy screen that separated them and sat.

She bowed her head and let her inner senses take control of her body. She reached out and touched each of the occupants of her palace. She touched Shen's mind and was surprised to find no shame in him. He seemed to be proud of the answers he had given to their people while verifying she was still a virgin. She sensed his love for her as his queen and his sister. She found in him the hope that she would succeed. She found his dislike of the Ah'Jarl, and saw that he realized it was based on misinformation taught by the wizards. She saw that Shen was struggling to overcome his dislike of the nomads, and how much his friendship with 'Ulan was helping. Shen might not like her Champion, but he trusted him to do what was best for her.

Mar'ya moved on and touched All'ya and the woman laughed and whispered, "Hello, my queen. Get out of my head and back into your own."

"Later, I would speak to you, All'ya," Mar'ya whispered, and then moved on.

So it went. In turn, she touched each inhabitant of the palace, paying close attention to the members of her council.

The desert folk recognized her touch and thought greetings and apologies to her. Rowan was the only member of the Crystal Guardians whose mind she dared to touch, and the woman's thoughts were clear and gentle.

"All is well, My Queen. We have faith in you."

"You will be trained, cousin, even if I must do it myself." Mar'ya vowed with a smile.

She left her Champion for last. When she reached out for his mind she found a barrier.

"'Quarl?"

"No, Mar'ya. I have told you that I would not betray you, but there must be trust between us."

"Blind trust? I am not ready for that. What hide you?"

"Secrets not for a woman to share. As you have secrets not to be shared with a man. I'll not trespass in your head, if you refrain from trying to peep into mine."

Mar'ya laughed softly and whispered back, "Oh, men's secrets? We shall see, my Champion. Do you know, in spite of everything, I am inclined to trust you?"

Mar'ya turned her attention to her own mind and tried to sort out the lifetime's accumulation of doubts and fears there.

She doubted her ability to be a good queen, that was true, but she would be better for Crystia than the western emperor ever could be.

As Mar'ya sorted through her mind, she was surprised at the amount of self-doubts she found. She had always thought of herself as a very self-confident, young woman. She was surprised to discover that many of her actions were based on her fear of failure.

She had bargained with Shen because of fear: Fear of the unknown and fear of failing to measure up as a woman. If she refused him, she had decided, then she would not truly become a woman. She could stay, in her mind anyway, still a child.

That was why she still threw temper tantrums. It was her way of saying to those around her. "See, I am still a child and not to be held accountable for my actions."

Her fear was why she had chosen the Ah'Jarl, a man she had never met, to be her Champion. She was afraid she couldn't measure up to the requirements of her noblemen. She had chosen one, that, in her heart, she considered inferior.

Crystal, what an unworthy daughter of the goddess she was. That had worked to the good, however. The goddess knew what her weakness would cause her to do. Her fear led her to take the action necessary to fulfill the prophecy of the stones. Understanding that, Mar'ya forgave herself and put it behind her.

She thought, with shame, of what the desert elders must have read in her heart when first she saw their Ah'Jarl, and of how she had briefly plotted to take 'Ulan away from them. No wonder they forced that new treaty on her people.

To win trust, she was beginning to see, one must first give trust. She only paid lip service to the desert people. She had not really trusted them. Deep inside, she expected the tribesmen to betray her in one way or another. Gradually,

Mar'ya began to forgive herself, seeing how each of her flaws brought her closer to the destiny the goddess planned for her. She relaxed and let her mind roam free. She passed over the camp of her half-brother, but did not stop, lest the wizards there detected her. She went to that place in the heart of the desert, where the four old women sat.

They smiled, "Welcome, Daughter, we were waiting for you."

They took her to the place where water fell in the heart of the desert and Mar'ya laughed in delight. She dove into the shallow pool at foot of the waterfall, and came up refreshed. Mar'ya felt as though the water washed away all her doubts and fears, leaving her clean and new, with sympathy and understanding for her weakness, and joy in her strength.

As she left that place, she felt the touch of another mind. One of the Wizard Council was scanning the psychic sphere and touched her. Quickly, she fled before him, knowing that she was not strong enough to face him alone.

She felt the wizard's surprise at her presence on that plane, then felt his laugh. He knew that she could not defeat him. They both knew that here, she was easy prey for his stronger will. Mar'ya twisted and turned, trying to evade the thin lines of power he weaved around her. She was becoming desperate, when, with a painful wrench, she found herself in another place.

"What are you doing here?" 'Quarl's voice was gentle in her mind.

She had gone to the place of warriors, where she completed the last phase of her training. She ignored his question and searched this place for what she needed. The two old men who had been her tutors came to her.

"This way, Little Queen," they said, leading her to a place of towering stones.

When she tried to approach the stones, they repelled her, yet this was where she must go. She knew it. Again and again, she battered her psyche against the unyielding stones until, tired and almost in tears, she retreated. Her quest was doomed so very close to success.

"Not so, Mar'ya. Come. I will show you the way," The Ah'Jarl said, "Some things can't be done alone."

Their minds merged, and together, they went to the great stones, and were accepted. A sense of contentment entered the joined being as the stones gifted them with the courage and strength of the mightiest of warriors.

Still joined, the witch and the warrior left that place and went back to the desert's heart. There, she showed him the mighty waterfall. This was her place, as the stones had been his. She understood that, as he had shared with her, it was now her turn to share with him.

As one, they dove into the placid pool and accepted the gift it gave them. The qualities of the stones were softened by compassion and understanding, both for themselves and for others. They stepped from the water, and found they had forged a bond between them that neither time nor death could destroy.

As they left that place, they sensed the mind of the enemy wizard still searching for the one he touched earlier.

They laughed joyfully, not trying to evade him. Together, they were invincible, as the wizards would discover when the time was right. Not yet, they agreed as they passed without drawing his attention. They were one, fire and ice joined, and the stones and the waterfall would be a part of their souls forever.

The terms of the Lady Crystal had been met. The whole Wizard Council would not be able to defeat them now.

Choosing the Ah'Jarl as her Champion was the will of the goddess, and had nothing to do with her silly, girlish fears. The two of them would hold this continent, this world if they so chose, and no one could make them slaves. No outside rulers would ever take their land so long as they and their children remained true to Crystal and Stone.

Back in the palace, Mar'ya returned to her body. Already she missed the warrior's presence. She acknowledged that the separation was only temporary and grinned across the room at him. He was her other half, as she was his, the friendship, the love and the passion that would one day burn between them would last for all eternity. They met at the door of the temple and joined hands, smiling at each other.

*****

The morning of the third day dawned clear and cool. Mar'ya and Quarl had not seen each other since they had left the temple two mornings earlier. Now, they met at the door of the Crystal Temple with the Crystal Guardians, the Lords of the faithful Houses, and the Desert Elders in attendance. There was no time for any conversation between them, but they smiled as they entered.

There, on the third day since the Lady had spoken, the witch and the warrior were joined, and proclaimed life-mates, according to laws of Stoneland Desert and of Crystia. As they bowed before the sliver of the Crystal that Burns, Crystal appeared. Standing beside her was the bright god of the desert, Stone.

Mar'ya stared at the two glowing figures, "Alex and Solari?" She whispered in surprise.

The two figures smiled gently. Crystal reached out and touched Mar'ya's hair, "Children, you have satisfied the prophecy," she said softly, "Because of you, my mate and I are once more joined. Know that we shall keep our word to you. At the height of the sun, go to the tower that looks out over the sea. Raise your arms and call us. We will answer, and with our help, you shall defeat our enemies.

"The two that had been sundered are now one. Long ago, we were one people, but the dark lord of the west betrayed us, and locked my love deep in the earth of Stoneland Desert. He sowed distrust in the hearts of our people and so divided us until the prophecy that Mist spoke should be fulfilled.

"The wizards who follow the dark god serve only to defeat the prophecy. However, they lost the knowledge of what the desert folk really were, so their plan to keep me separated for all time from the one I love, has failed. Your victory shall be ours. Our blessings on you and all your children for as long as they keep faith with us."

*****

The Queen Mar'ya, House Sultav, Witch, and Holder of the Crystal Throne, and her Champion, 'Quarl the Ah'Jarl, Warrior Mage of all the Desert Tribes, climbed the stairs to the palace tower overlooking the sea.

The wind whipped their clothes and their hair. Mar'ya held tightly to 'Quarl's hand trying to keep her feet on the floor. Slowly, they made their way to the edge of the tower. Once there, they looked down on the camp of their enemies and sent their challenge to the wizards below.

"Behold, the two that were separated are now joined; Stone and Crystal are one. Your plots have failed. Go back to your dark god and tell him that this land is no longer unprotected."

When the wizards heard this, they cried aloud in fear and rage. Their god would not be pleased with their failure. In desperation, they joined their minds and sent a blast of destructive power toward the two on the tower.

The queen and her champion lifted their arms and deflected the wizard's magic, sending the force far out to sea, where it turned the sky gray and lifted the water high against the horizon.

Emperor Gregor watched the exchange. When he felt the pressure in his head lighten, he realized that, with the wizards' attention focused on the two challengers, he was free of their control. He sent a quick blessing to the challengers and turned to his captains, ordering his army pulled back to their ships. He had a feeling that this battle was not going at all the way the wizards planned it, and wanted his men out of harm's way. This war would be won or lost by magic, and it was no place for his soldiers. He gave no thought to his allies from the city. They dealt with the wizards, let the wizards protect them now.

Mar'ya and 'Quarl felt the power of the wizards beating against their minds. They lifted their joined hands high. Lightning came from the sky to touch their fingers. They deflected that power into the very heart of the wizards' circle.

From the desert came a hot, dry wind: From Crystal Mountain, a cold, damp one. They met where the wizards stood. Mar'ya and 'Quarl stood on the tower and watched the scene below them with awe. The meeting of the two winds caused a tremendous storm. Lightning flashed, thunder rolled. The screams of men and riding beasts could be heard above the noise of the storm. The ocean pulled back, carrying the ships of the westerners far away from the shore, then paused, as the ships moved away from the developing wall of water that roared back to the beach. The very earth shuddered under the force of its return as it buried land, trees, and humans. The water smashed against the walls of Crystal City. The great walls shuddered and held, while an eerie silence descended on the land.

From the direction of the western lands came Storm in the shape of a huge, black cloud. When the cloud reached the shore, it hovered for an instant then attacked the witch and the warrior with a force that drove them to their knees. The awesome power of a god beat upon their minds, and darkness covered them. In the midst of the darkness, walked flame-haired Crystal. Beside her, his eyes gleaming, walked Stone. They stood beside their chosen and lifted Mar'ya and 'Quarl to their feet.

"We are with you. Our strength is yours for the asking." The two gods whispered in Mar'ya's and 'Quarl's minds.

In unison, the witch and the warrior cried out, calling upon the gods of their land, "Crystal, Stone, aid us in this our hour of need."

Strength poured into their bodies as they pushed the darkness away, forcing the storm cloud back to the west and away from their lands forever. The battle raged for minutes that were days, and for a moment, they thought they had failed, then the pressure on their minds ceased. The dark cloud coiled into itself and fled back to the west from where it had come.

Mar'ya and 'Quarl stood on the tower, and watched until the storm had worn itself out. Far in the distance, Mar'ya saw the ships of Emperor Gregor driven westward by an angry wind. Of the Houses that had betrayed her, there was no sign. Mar'ya hoped that the emperor had taken them with him, but somehow, she didn't think he had.

Mar'ya shook the rain out of her eyes, leaned against the wall of the tower, tried to steady her shaking knees, and stared at the scene below. The walls of the palace now stood at the edge of a steep cliff. Where Crystal Harbor once stood, angry waves beat against the sides of the cliff. Instead of sitting in the middle of a wide plain, Crystal City was perched high above the landscape, dominating the scene for miles around. She shuddered to think what the rest of land must look like.

She glanced at 'Quarl, and saw by the shocked look on his face that his thoughts must be close to her own. She whispered a brief prayer that the people outside the walls were safe. "We must go to the Hall of Judgment. Now."

"Why the rush? We are both exhausted."

"It is the will of the goddess. Judgment should be rendered quickly, fairly, and according to her laws. We will have plenty of time to rest later"

"Will you go as you are, in those wet clothes?"

"Yes. I can change later. This will not take long."

"What of my people?"

"Need you ask 'Quarl? They are our people now. I will deal with them fairly, I promise."

Mar'ya gave him a quick smile, then entered the Hall of Judgment and took her place at the head of the long table.

She looked at her people standing in respect waiting for her to begin the judging. "The time of battle is over, the enemy is defeated. The time of healing is now begun."

The room was silent as Mar'ya sat on the Crystal Throne for the first time in her life. 'Quarl took the seat on her right, then the rest of their people sat.

"The following judgment is passed on the people of the Crystal Kingdom: The Warrior Houses, Avil and Sul are no more.

"The Farming Houses of the East Eva, and Hai are no more.

"The Northern Mining Houses Sna, Ika, and Slee are no more.

"The Southern Hunters, Des, Util and Wara, are no more.

"The Western Fishing Houses Fi, Oc, and Wav are no more.

"These Houses have been judged and declared traitors to their queen and their goddess. The wealth of these Houses, their lands, and their goods, shall be divided among the faithful. The children of these Houses shall be adopted, and all memory of the traitors shall be erased from the mind of Crystal for eternity.

"People of Stoneland Desert: Before the Crystal Lady and the Stone Lord, you have been judged, and named forsworn. These are your punishments: One: All women of power in the Crystal Kingdom will be trained in your holy places, along with your own women. Two: Two of your best swordsmen will live in the city and train all who ask, be they male or female, in the art of fighting. Three: Your finest warriors will live in the city as a part of the queen's own guard. Four: Your elders shall abide in Crystal

City half of every year. Five: The first-born son of each tribe's chief will be sent to Crystal City, in their sixteenth year. They will live among my people and learn our ways, so there will never again be war between us.

"This is the Judgment of Crystal and Stone, does any here dissent?" Mar'ya waited a moment. When the room remained silent, she nodded. "Then the judgment is complete, let it stand as I have said until the sun no longer shines, and the wind no longer blows."

She held her hand to 'Quarl, and together, they left the Judgment Hall.

She was tired, but it was a good feeling. There were so many plans to be made, so much to be done, she thought, as she ran up the stairs to her room, but it would wait. Now, she would let her House Lords and Desert Chiefs take care of things. She and 'Quarl parted company at the head of the stairs, for their rooms were on opposite ends of the hallway, *I will have to arrange for us to move into the royal suite sometime soon. Maybe Mase can take care of that for me. I am so tired right now, I could sleep for a year, and there is still so much left to do*. She shook her wet hair and opened the door to her chambers, then stopped in surprise.

"Alex, Solari, what are you two doing here?"

Alex stretched his long legs out in front of him, and Solari, sitting in the chair next to his, smiled. "We have come to tell you goodbye. You have done very well, and we are very proud of you." Solari said softly. "I also need to tell you that young Trina has been cleansed of the wizards' taint. Crystal gave her the gift of forgetfulness, and the young witch in training is making Shen's life miserable."

Mar'ya grinned maliciously, "Good. It gives me great joy when my cousins receive all they deserve." She frowned and stared hard at Alex and Solari. "Who are you really?" She asked cautiously.

"How soon the young forget," Alex drawled, "For the last six years, I have been your beloved cousin and errand boy. Now you ask who I am? My heart is broken."

Mar'ya smiled in relief, it really was Alex. "Where are you going?"

"A lot has changed on our continent, I am going to check on the desert nomads, and any of our people who might have survived outside the walls. Solari will be at House Frya helping with the refugees. We will be sending you reports about once a month."

"Alex, be careful."

"Always, Sweet Cousin. You will not get rid of me easily. By the way, how much longer will you be staying in these rooms? You have a husband now, don't you think it's time you moved?"

Mar'ya scowled, "I have had a lot on my mind, and I've only been wed a few hours."

"So, where are the two of you going on your wedding trip?" Solari asked, then she and Alex laughed at the stunned look on Mar'ya's face.

By the time Mar'ya regained her composure, her cousins had left the room. She sighed, wondered where Mase was, shed her wet clothes, and crawled naked into her bed.

It was dark when Mase's voice woke her, "Look at you: Wet hair, and no bedclothes on. What are you doing in this room? I moved you and your hulk of husband into the Royal Chambers this morning. His man and I have been waiting for you two all day."

"Mase, I'm tired and cold. Why did you pull my covers off?" Mar'ya grumbled.

Mase threw her arms up, "There are no covers. The bed is not even made."

"Then why were Alex and Solari in here waiting for me?" Mar'ya was beginning to wake up.

Mase frowned, "Are you running a fever? Alex and Solari left the city two days ago. Don't you remember?" Mase reached out and touched Mar'ya's cheeks, "I wouldn't be surprised if you were feverish, sleeping with wet hair and no covers."

Mase removed her cloak, wrapped it around Mar'ya and led her gently down the hall to her new rooms where 'Quarl was fast asleep in one of the chairs. Mase led Mar'ya to the bed, and pulled a nightgown over her head, "Now, sit and let me dry your hair." She commanded.

"Mase, don't fuss. Tomorrow will be soon enough, I just want to sleep." Mar'ya mumbled, and fell asleep before Mase could get her covered.

Mar'ya awoke early the next morning, grabbed the breeches and tunic she had worn in the desert and pulled them on.

"Mase, where is 'Quarl?" she asked as she glanced around the sitting room that divided the two bedrooms of the royal suite.

"Said he was going to the western tower, and that you should meet him there," Mase frowned at Mar'ya, "You are not going anywhere dressed like that..." the slamming of the door cut her statement short.

'Quarl smiled at the gamin figure of the greatest witch in their land, barefoot and hair in total disarray, "Sleepyhead." He chided gently.

Mar'ya frowned at him, but before she could protest further, he silenced her by placing a finger over her lips.

Holding hands, they walked to the edge of the tower. From there, they looked out over the land the gods had put in their care.

"You were gentle with my people."

"Our people," she corrected. "And they won't think that when the first lot of Crystia's women begin training. We are a difficult group."

She leaned on the wall surrounding the tower and breathed deeply of the clean storm-washed air. "It's not over yet. There are still members of the traitorous Houses to be dealt with. There will also be those left homeless because of the changes. They will need to be relocated."

"We'll manage." 'Quarl put his arms around her shoulders.

"Yes. Yes we will." She said leaning into his embrace.

Mar'ya sighed in contentment. This was her Champion, her mate for life. The future held a lot of problems. Bringing their people together would not be easy, but she trusted 'Quarl and the gods.

Epilogue

High in the mountains, Mist shook out her hair and smiled at her friends, "I will leave you now." She whispered.

"Where are you going?" Flame-haired Crystal asked.

"To the west. Storm has been alone too long and the western people will need me to protect them from his wrath."

"Are you sure?" Crystal frowned.

"Am I sure about what?" Mist laughed. "You and Stone have each other, and Storm knows that he can no longer separate you. His people acted honorably, except for the wizards, and they are no more. I can stop him from starting up that nasty group again. I can soften his anger. Storm belongs to me as Stone belongs to you. I will go to him and remind him of that. Don't worry. He will not harm me."

"You still love him?" Crystal hugged Mist.

"Oh yes," Mist floated away, "For all eternity." She whispered on the breeze as she disappeared over the western horizon.